My Mother's Lover

THE SWISS LIST

My Mother's Lover
URS WIDMER

TRANSLATED BY DONAL MCLAUGHLIN

LONDON NEW YORK CALCUTTA

swiss arts council

prohelvetia

This publication was supported by a grant from
Pro Helvetia, Swiss Arts Council

Seagull Books, 2017

© Urs Widmer, 2000
First published by Diogenes Verlag AG, Zürich, 2003

English translation © Donal McLaughlin

First published in English translation by Seagul Books, 2011

ISBN 978 0 8574 2 526 3

British Library Cataloguing-in-Publication Data
A catalogue record for this book is available
from the British Library

Typeset by Seagull Books, Calcutta, India
Printed by Hyam Enterprises, Calcutta, India

For Nora

MY mother's lover died today. As old as the hills he was, and fit as a fiddle even as he died. He was bent over a lectern and turning the page of a score—Mozart's Symphony in G minor—when he collapsed. When they found him, he was clutching a scrap of music: the horn at the start of the slow movement. He'd once told my mother the Symphony in G minor was the most beautiful piece of music ever composed. — He'd always read scores the way others read books. Everything and anything he could get his hands on, be it archaic, or superficial. He looked out, above all, for *new* work. Only in his old age, at about ninety, did the urge take him to re-read familiar pieces, differently this time, in the light of the fading sun that was his life. He now read *Don Giovanni* again, which he'd devoured with burning eyes as a young man; and *The Creation*. — He'd been a musician, a conductor. Three days

1

before he died, he conducted his final concert in the Stadthalle. György Ligeti, Bartók, Conrad Beck. — My mother loved him all her life. Not that he noticed. That anyone noticed. No one knew of her passion, not a word did she ever speak on the subject. 'Edwin,' mind you, she would whisper when she stood alone at the lake, holding her child's hand. There, in the shade, surrounded by quacking ducks, she'd look across at the sunlit shore opposite. 'Edwin!' The conductor's name was Edwin.

HE was a good conductor. The richest person in the country when he died. He owned the most valuable collection of scores far and wide; the page he'd torn as he died had been an original. He held the majority of shares in a conglomerate that manufactured, and still does, machines, mostly. Locomotives, ships, but also looms and turbines and, lately, even the high-precision instruments used in laser surgery. Artificial joints, and those mini-cameras that can be sent through the bloodstream to the heart and transmit whatever they find on to a screen. The head office of the company was, and still is, on that less desirable side of the lake that is always in the shade. Edwin, on the other hand, lived on the sunny side, above the lake, in an estate with thirty or even fifty rooms, stud farms, dog kennels, with guest houses and servants' quarters in a park where Chinese stone pines and sequoia trees grew, sky-high whoppers, in whose shade he would stroll, memorizing his next concert. At the Royal Albert Hall, for example, or

Glyndebourne. For his concerts he demanded a princely sum, but not because he was after money, yet more money, but because he measured himself against Bruno Walter and Otto Klemperer. He wanted the same fee, and he got it.

ONCE, as a young man, he'd been as poor as a church mouse. Had lived in a furnished room in the industrial part of town, raging with ambition and a talent that had yet to unfold. There would be flashes in his head as he pounded up and down, bumping against chairs and wash bowls, not that he noticed, as he chased the elusive, wild music in his skull. Sometimes, he poured ice-cold water over himself. He had music paper in all his pockets, and on walks that were more like hurried forced marches, he'd write down bits of melody, though barely familiar with notation. His ability to play the piano was even sketchier. But he lived *in* music, and *for* music. Back then —prices were scary, even in those days—he'd turn up at the subscription concerts at the interval, when tickets were no longer being checked, and the most fatigued of the melomaniacs had already left. He'd proceed to take their seats, enduring the deadly looks from the people next to him. And so, each time, he heard the second half at least. It was always Brahms, Beethoven, Bruckner in any case. Not having the required qualifications, he wasn't eligible for the Konservatorium. So he asked a local composer to give him tuition, someone who, when Edwin described his meagre means, also waived the fee. The man in question worked only in patches,

3

mind you—he drank, if truth be told—and was a fanatical follower of Richard Wagner and Richard Strauss. Of all the Richards, actually. François Richard he liked more, too, than the man in question merited. He sang the latter's 'Ruisseau qui cours après toy-mesme' at almost every lesson, accompanying himself on the piano with powerful octaves, though the original required a delicate lute.—Years later, many years later, Edwin could have bought the score, at auction, for next to nothing. He joined in the bidding, if hesitantly, initially, then let a fat, heavily perspiring gentleman, representing the J. Paul Getty Foundation for Ancient Music, have it.—He recreated the work of Gesualdo, trembled over the marvels of Mozart, endured Schubert's longueurs, and was soon composing his own first piece, a two-movement symphony which had the local composer shaking his head as he read it. When that first blaze of composition faded, he learned to play the piano (something the local composer really knew about). He wasn't able to practise, though—how should he, when he didn't have a piano—or was only able to when the composer had had too much to drink, and was sleeping it off in the next room. And so he remained someone for whom even slow movements were too fast. Despairing already, the local composer showed him, one day, how to conduct. How to give a proper upbeat, or produce a ritardando, everything like that. He knew all the techniques, the local composer. Even if he was drunk, or especially then, he would beat time without the slightest problem—a 6/9 rhythm with his left hand, and a 5/8 with his right. Edwin discovered, to his own and his teacher's

4

amazement that—at the drop of a hat almost—he could do this too. He knew right away: he was born to conduct. He worked his way through the complete works of Johann Sebastian Bach, Haydn and Mendelssohn—the local composer, at the piano, took the place of the orchestra; later through all of Debussy even. His interpretation of *Pelléas and Mélisande* was so intense that when he, later, got to play it with a real orchestra, he was desperately sad as that performance didn't sound nearly as splendid as the imagined one. One bright summer morning, his master told him he'd taught him all he could! He hugged him. Edwin left. He didn't turn back and so didn't see the local composer at the window, one hand raised to wave to him, the other holding a bottle.—He whistled to himself. He still wasn't able to compose, true. And his piano-playing was still lamentable. But if he read a score, he could *hear* it, and he was now a dab hand at conducting too.—He'd been able to keep himself by painting shutters on a piecework basis, by waiting at tables in a garden cafe and by sorting the mail at the main post office. His studies, after all, hadn't cost him anything.

EDWIN poor; my mother, however, rich—that's how it was, to begin with. Only later was the situation reversed. By then, Edwin was swimming in it, and my mother, now struggling, talked more and more about how she'd end up in a poorhouse. —As a young woman, my mother, a dazzling beauty, had wafted up, as if in a dream. Long legs and high heels, serious, black eyes, full lips, a fur round her shoulders, a hat the size of a cartwheel, a frizzy mane pouring out from under it. Feathers. Alongside her sprang a greyhound. — At the subscription concerts, she sat beside her father, in Mother's place — the latter having died when my mother was a teenager — devastatingly young amidst all the hoary old subscribers, who looked dead. Even her father wouldn't seem very alive, and the concert would barely have started when my mother, every time, would have the urge to scream out. To raise the dead. — Her father looked like Verdi as an old man, a Verdi with big lips, did, in fact, love *La Traviata* more than anything else, and he was the deputy director of the very factory that was later — not so very much later at this stage! — to pass to Edwin. He wouldn't have dared, Edwin, to speak to my mother back then. She, if he had, would've looked right through him, forgetting him even as she did. Back then, that is. — From time to time she'd watched him, from up in her balcony as, after the interval, he looked for a seat in the stalls, a shabbily dressed young man, both helpless *and* determined. She'd thought nothing more of it.

ONCE, at the age of five or six, she was playing in the hall with her dolls — teaching them how to behave properly — when the study door opened and her father stood in the doorway, his eyes flashing, his lips forming a thin line, his beard resembling a shovel. With this very beard, he pointed into the room. My little mother entered, hesitantly, and her bare feet sank into the rug as she stood before the iron desk, behind which her father—darkening the window—towered. Books with dark covers wherever she looked, dim lamps with glass-bead tassels, Greek marble busts of Zeus or Apollo, test tubes, a terrarium in which scorpions and garden spiders were crawling. Her father stood there, saying nothing, looked at her, looked and looked, and finally, through closed lips, said 'No one wants you! No one! And it's because of your manner!' He let out a roar, suddenly. 'Get to your room!' he shouted. 'I don't want to set eyes on you!'—He and his wife had wanted to go to Milan. Good hotel, good food, nice wines, *La Traviata* at *La Scala*, maybe. *Tosca*, at least. But no one had been willing to take my little mother for a few days, not a single aunt, cousin, godmother or friend. 'That one? Never!' Not even Alma, whom people approached only in a real emergency, had been prepared to look after her. Because of her manner. Her parents had stayed at home.—My mother went to her room. Stood at the window without a tear, wondering what her manner was. The fact that even her father and her mother didn't want her.—She didn't shed a tear in later years, either. Her eyes were so dry, they hurt.

ANOTHER time, at the age of six, and then, again, at eight, she didn't want to finish her meal. Spinach, cauliflower, some kind of healthy mush like that. Yoghurt! Made by the maid, sometimes by Mama herself. At times like this, her father insisted she eat everything, every last drop. Even if it took her

7

three days. Or a whole year. She'd often sit alone in her room, the yoghurt in front of her, the walls of her stomach rigid. Not a bite could she get down. Her father, at the next meal, wouldn't so much as look at her, would eat his steak with stony pleasure. Before her on the table: the half-eaten yoghurt still. Mould wasn't poisonous, not for children. — Just once, a single once, had she tried, behind his back, to put the yoghurt in a vase. Her father, all-knowing, had reached in, shown her his yoghurt-covered finger, and wiped it, without a word, on his serviette. Next thing she knew, a new yoghurt was in front of her. — She attended kindergarten, and then school. And if she wasn't home fifteen minutes after school ended, her father would lock the door. She'd stand there, ringing the bell and shouting, until her father opened the flap—a barred window, behind which he looked like a prison guard who, for some reason, was in the jail itself while the prisoner outside begged to get in. He'd say, calmly and clearly, that she'd arrived late, that she'd just have to wait until the gate opened again, when-ever that might be, not right now, certainly, anyway. And she'd her manner to thank for that. — On one occasion, the time was just up—no, she was late, a minute late, for sure— her father had bolted the door though she was already on her way up the garden. Too late was too late. And so she sat on the front step, watching a squirrel in the pine tree jump from branch to branch. Her manner, her manner, —what was her manner?

MAYBE her manner was the way she often stood, rigid, in the corner of a room, her eyes focused inward, her fists clenched, and with a burning heat in her head. She would hardly breathe at moments like that, would groan from time to time. Inwardly, boiling; for the outside world, she was but skin, and dead. Deaf, blind. You could've carried her away like a piece of wood, like a coffin, and she wouldn't have noticed. She'd have died of shame, right enough, if you'd taken her unawares, rigid like this. She'd have got the fright of her life, and felt guilty. That was why she listened out for the slightest noise in the house, a door opening somewhere, maybe, footsteps in the hall, any creaking or rustling. But no one ever discovered her secret, of that she was certain. — (That said, on more than one occasion, she stared right through her parents, who didn't rouse her, didn't dare.) — Deep inside her, at moments like this, was a world that dazzled and shone, with woods, cornfields, with paths leading off in different directions. Butterflies, glow-worms. Horsemen in the distance. She retreated into herself too, watched herself hopping, doing cartwheels, shrieking with delight. She wore delightful little outfits, ribbons, white shoes, a straw hat full of cornflowers. Everyone loved her, yes, she was everyone's favourite. She wasn't the queen, or only rarely was she the queen, no, she was unrivalled when it came to being unassuming, and shared everything she had with the poorest of the poor. She kept only the things she really needed. The pony, of course, and the four-poster bed. She often cried with the others — in *that* world, she did have tears — because things were going so badly for them. She would comfort them,

9

had a great ability to comfort people. People always came to her, pushing and shoving they'd be to get to her. Outstretched arms, pleading, her name being called. She could magic herself free, mind you, would then be all alone, would walk on water, was even able to fly. She'd be close to the stars at moments like this, would call to them, and they'd laugh back, in reply. God, —with God she'd no dealings; but sometimes Little Jesus would come up to her and ask for advice about the future of the world. And so, from time to time, she was required to be a stern judge too. Would stand in a gallery above a church-like room full of black men who had committed or planned evil deeds. And yes, indeed, she'd no option but to boil them in oil. Chop their heads off, or cast them from the tower—there was no way round it. Their pleas for mercy didn't help, not at all, all this shifting around on their knees and wringing of hands in a bid to receive her forgiveness. She remained just, gave them the thumbs-down. —Something or other would then rouse her, a dog, maybe, barking in the street, or a floorboard creaking (her parents creeping away). And she'd start, look around, distraught, come to her senses again. —Then at supper, her Mama, wide-eyed. What was wrong? Why was her father looking at her like that?

THE latter hadn't always lived amid busts of antique gods and Persian rugs. On the contrary: he'd come into the world in a house with no furniture, not much more than a pile of stone, near Domodossola, an infant, the colour of stone pine that, already at birth, had hair like steel wool and those lips. He was the youngest of twelve children—all of whom also had frizzy hair and fat lips—and was christened Ultimo. His parents begged God: enough was enough, please. (Of the twelve children, just five reached adulthood.) He went around with no shoes, looked for chestnuts in the forest, fed grass to the rabbits. The house, crouched beneath a rock, consisted of *one* room, a deep, windowless vault, in which, in winter, a fire blazed beneath a huge maw of a chimney, but barely warmed the air. In the summer, on the other hand, the vault was cool even if, outside, the sun was scorching. The sons, seven of them, helped their father. Only Ultimo wasn't allowed to, his father didn't need an eighth labourer; not one so small, anyway. Ultimo had to stay at home. He didn't know *exactly* what his father and brothers did, their adventures involved mules somehow, and sleighs and carts. He thought they were something like good robbers, that they descended on the castles of evil lords on the other side of the mountains, and gave what they stole to the poor. Oh, how he'd have liked to do so too! Getting up at five, and back after sunset, exhausted, sweaty, with bad cuts sometimes, and tales of adventures in which avalanches had thundered down on them, or rocks. The mules had scarpered, raced off up the mountain, braying, and dragging the sleighs behind them, from which some barrels broke free and thundered into the valley, bursting as they crashed, and turning the snow blood red. Their father sat at the table and looked on, beaming, as their mother scraped polenta into the amazing brothers' plates. He'd had to laugh so hard, he was wiping away tears. Ultimo, all the while, in his dark corner, having eaten already. — Their father was a mule driver, led sumpter mules over the mountain. Hired by wine-growers from Piedmont, he transported casks of wine over the Simplon Pass, between Domodossola and Brig. In winter on sleighs, and in summer on carts. His sons helped him, seven sons in their prime; soon to be just three. The others had died, typhoid fever, polio, blood poisoning. Ultimo, though, wasn't allowed to replace them; not one of them, ever. Maybe one day, when his father was old and struggling to persuade his eldest to go over the pass with him, him and the team, maybe then he'd be allowed to, Ultimo. By then, however, he was long since elsewhere. In another country, with other friends, and with new money.

LUCKILY, he was good at school, Ultimo. The teacher in the village noticed, some clergyman or other got involved, the priest in the parish of Villa di Domodossola, and suddenly the talented Ultimo found himself beyond the pass, on the other side of the mountains. He was now a pupil at the Jesuit boarding school in Brig. This saintly school may have instilled in him a lifelong loathing of all things religious—later, he stopped going to Mass and didn't have his daughter baptized—but he learned a lot. A singsong variety of German and prayers in Latin, but also adding, subtracting, how to draw things, classify things, how to shuffle and separate out, how to dissect beetles, and calculate the side of a cube that has the same volume as a cone. His results in his leaving certificate were quite brilliant. The ceremony took place in the cathedral. A few hundred attended, touched by what they witnessed. A bishop, or some other member of the church's top brass, said some prayers and handed the certificates out, then said some more prayers, and even patted Ultimo's hair as he gave him his certificate. That was the last time Ultimo saw the inside of a church. Later, when he travelled with his wife—to Chartres, Autun, Vézelay—he always waited outside the portal while she marvelled her way through the crypts and the cloisters.—He attended the national polytechnic (received a grant, though a foreigner), qualified as an engineer and, having just turned twenty-four, went into that factory on the dark side of the lake. It was small and dilapidated at that point: a few sheds in which large-calibre screws were manufactured, right- and left-hand threads, metal spindles, springs and brake chocks. Ultimo sat in an office, a wooden shed, processing the few orders they had. He married and had a daughter, my mother. Then the First World War came along. The warring factions, on both sides, needed so many machines (shot so many to pieces) that four years later the firm was a large concern and Ultimo one of its deputy directors. He was responsible for the production of military vehicles, a department that was growing rapidly. He now earned a lot of money, built a house, wore flannels from England, had a maid, had the cheese, the dried beef, the polenta, and the wine from where he grew up delivered to him, bought a gramophone, and sat there, every evening, with a sherry in his hand, enraptured by how Caruso sang 'La donna è mobile'. He smoked cigars. Registered as a citizen of his new home town. Bought one of the first cars in the town, a Barbera-red Fiat, a Cabriolet, that he fetched from Turin himself. The seats, the dashboard, everything was fitted to his specifications. He drove over the mountains, singing (avoiding the Simplon Pass as he feared the spirit of his — now long dead — father and the ghosts of the mules). He changed three wheels, scalded himself when, naively, he unscrewed the radiator to check the water. With a burned chin and bandaged hands, and radiant despite everything that had happened to him, he steered his wonder vehicle through forests, gorges, villages — leaving clouds of dust behind him. He arrived home in the light of the setting sun; was met by his wife and his little daughter with flowers. Smiling, he took off his goggles and leather cap and dust coat. Neighbours, peering through their fences, vanished — like lizards into their holes — when he waved to them. Wasn't life beautiful! — Then his wife died, his daughter grew up and became an adult, that unexpected beauty, and he turned to stone. He no longer spoke, hardly ate. Many a night, he stayed up all night, listening to that Johann Sebastian Bach cantata in which the bass-baritone, singing wonderfully, greets his own death. He stopped buying new clothes; buying anything at all, actually. He would turn every light in the house off, and air all the rooms. On 26 October 1929, the day after Black Friday, he opened his morning paper to read that he'd lost all his money. From one day to the next, he was poor again. He got up from his easy-chair, his mouth opened, and reaching for his heart, he crashed to the ground. There he lay, on a precious rug, in a purple dressing-gown, his head between the leaves of the palm tree he'd knocked over. His glassy eyes were looking towards the window, outside which the sun had yet to rise. His dressing-gown had fallen open, he was lying naked on his back. His skin, once the colour of stone pine wood, now shone like old copper. That was how my mother found him. She covered him up, released the crushed paper from his fingers, and read the news that killed him. Only some time later, though, did she comprehend that, for her now too, this rich lifestyle was over. For the moment, she simply stared, both fists tight against her lips, at this suddenly strange man who, in death, resembled an Oriental prince, waiting to be paid his final homage.

HER father's father, you see, the mule driver, had had a much darker complexion. The reason for that was that *his* father had been black, an African from a highland below the equator, and all of this in an alpine valley where no one else realized there were people on the other side of the mountains. He didn't have a name, this black forefather. Everyone called him the Negro. Even his wife, my mother's father's father's mother, did, but not because she denied her short-lived love for him — which had lasted a single night. On the contrary: all her life, she made a cult of the missing man. Had a small altar with a candle on it that was always burning, and that shone, as she didn't have a picture of him, on a curious something-or-the-other the Negro had worn on a string round his neck. A tooth? A talon? She would kneel for hours before the eternal flame, kiss the relic, call out his name, the only name she had for him. 'Negro!' — Famine had forced the Negro to leave his country, as had tribal feuds. He, like all his tribe, was tall and lean, their victorious rivals were small and sturdy. They envied the lean tribe their dates company, and also had a different religion. *Their* god was a dog, the lean tribe's god was a lion. Their dignitaries, the initiated, always wore a part of a lion on their person, a hair from a tail, a paw, a jawbone. Just like their totem, they hounded buffalo and gnus to death, pursuing them for hours, days, if necessary, until their victims surrendered. No one knows how the Negro made it to Europe, whether he came ashore in Genoa, or perhaps more likely Livorno, or why he choose to go straight ahead, without stopping, and with nothing to eat or drink, bypassing villages with barking dogs, crossing cornfields and vineyards, and entering, finally, that rocky valley that climbed steeply, straight towards the highest of the icy peaks glowing in the light of evening. He was panting, staggering, could barely see where he was going. He passed a few houses — piles of rock, rather — and collapsed. Lay there, unconscious. And that was how a young woman found him. Walking backwards, she dragged him home by the legs. Light had by now completely faded. In the dark, she undressed him, gave him water, washed him. To warm him up, she snuggled up to him, dried him with towels, and spoke to him. 'Wake up! Go on, wake up!' She hugged, she kissed, she pleaded. She'd never smelled skin like it. Dear God in heaven, she prayed, let him come back to life, into my life. — At some point, when the night was at its darkest, the Negro moved, and the groans that followed were so distressing, and the sighs so sore, that the woman redoubled her efforts. No one knows what exactly happened that night, no one saw the couple that couldn't see itself. But they cried out, they howled, everyone heard that. They rollicked. They laughed, even! Then, towards morning, they fell silent, and maybe the others fell asleep, too, in their beds. In any case, when the sun came through the cracks in the door and shone on the lovers, the woman was sleeping, sprawled out, naked, on her back, her breathing gentle, her dreaming face smiling, her arms and legs wide apart. The Negro was dead. His mouth was open, his eyes, wide open, full of tears. Helpless, the others in the dwelling gathered round the couple, not daring to waken the woman, or to touch the dead man. Finally, an old man — the woman's father? — took heart and covered them both with his jacket — The woman buried the Negro, her one night of happiness, beneath a chestnut tree at the side of the house. Nine months later, she gave birth to a son, whom she called Domenico. — And so it came to be that my mother's father's father's father was black, my mother's father's father brown, my mother's father a copper colour, and my mother still someone, at least, who — as you could see — enjoyed the sun.

EDWIN was now a conductor, but one without an orchestra. For someone like him, the rostrum of the Philharmonic was further away than the moon. And so he created his own orchestra by persuading everyone he came across, able to play an instrument, to play for him. For the most part, these were young men and women, pupils at the Konservatorium; no one over twenty-five, anyway, by the time he got his crew together. No one, with the exception of a violinist who was coming up for sixty—Edwin made him the leader—and who had just left the Philharmonic over a quarrel. There'd been a discussion at a rehearsal about the performability of new music, and he'd had the audacity to contradict the principal conductor—an especially dry music officer who was to remain in this post for many decades—when your man claimed not one *playable* piece of music had been written since the turn of the century. And what about Korngold? the violinist had called out. Huber? Bartók!—He was fired on the spot.—For that reason, the first concert of the Young Orchestra—the name given by Edwin to his new ensemble—opened with the Suite op. 4 by Béla Bartók. The Concerto for Piccolo and Strings by Alexander von Zemlinsky followed. This ended up in the programme because one of Edwin's closest friends— and, for the moment, the only wind player in the orchestra— was a flautist, a young virtuoso with a special love of the piccolo. The concert closed with the world premiere of the local composer's Cinq Variations sur le thème Le ruisseau qui cours après toy-mesme de François Richard. Edwin had absolutely wanted a world premiere and found no other composer ready and able to write something for him in so short a time. The local composer had been delighted by Edwin's inquiry and, in the night that followed, had filled five to ten sheets of music paper with his eccentric script. As things turned out, he'd not then added to that, with the result that Edwin finally contented himself with these outlines, managed somehow or other to order the sheets of music, and orchestrated the voices as best he could — the notes, in any case, were barely legible. As he'd no wind players at his disposal — the flautist, after all, was the soloist — the murmuring of the eponymous little stream had to be played by the double basses. — The rehearsals were relentless. Anyone arriving late felt the full force of Edwin's wrath, anyone who hadn't learned his part properly, even more so. Edwin was so strict, indeed, that — by the third day of rehearsals — his musicians, the women in particular, were already singing his praises. Rehearsals at the crack of dawn — the pupils had to attend, of course, their classes at the music school — rehearsals deep into the night: they looked up to Edwin with more and more devotion. He was so confident! On the day of the concert, their nerves were all on edge, they all knew that today something significant would happen. Even the leader of the orchestra, an old hand, had a strange feeling in the pit of his stomach. The concert took place on 12 June 1926 in the Historical Museum. The audience — okay, there were a few at the back, above all, who'd just turned up — consisted of the artists' mothers and fathers, of their fiancés and fiancées, aunts, uncles, godparents, friends of every description. In

Bartók's Suite op. 4, Edwin lost his place right at the beginning, and the leader of the orchestra had to drag his colleagues through the next bar. Shortly after that, on the other hand, the leader of the orchestra and, with him, the first violins came in at the wrong place, and Edwin had to concede. The piece met with confused silence. An old man at the back shouted a timid boo. My mother didn't like the piece either. (She'd been lured along by a cellist, her best friend, a woman who went on to have a career in Berlin, and was then murdered in Buchenwald.) At the end of the Zemlinsky, those booing up at the back became braver and, red in the face, made their displeasure evident. But there was also applause for the soloist. After the Cinq Variations, however, real chaos erupted. Those at the back booed, howled, and whistled on keys, while those at the front clapped even harder, their bravos getting louder and louder. The local composer, who'd spent the entire concert in the cloakroom, could barely be persuaded on to the stage—and almost fell as he bowed. At this, his first concert, Edwin was as composed as he, later, always would be. At most, he bowed his head. Such was the thunderous applause that Edwin—in defiance of those booing, and to the great joy of those applauding—encored two of the Variations, the fourth and the fifth, in which the little stream finally floods the heart of the woman in love and, to the wooing of ever shriller cellos, she opens up. (The Fifth Variation was to become a much-requested piece, providing the local composer with a regular income.) Of course, not a single critic from either of the town's two newspapers was in the hall, though they'd been invited. This was perhaps also a good thing, though: by next morning, word was already spreading about the Orchestra. Everyone wanted to attend the concerts, be it just to boo and whistle. When the critics finally did want to come—further concerts followed, of course—Edwin no longer wanted them there. Not ever did a critic who hadn't purchased a ticket attend a concert by the Young Orchestra.—Afterwards, everyone—the artists, the fathers and mothers, the fiancés and fiancées, the god-parents, the aunts and uncles and friends, and even the local composer!—congregated in the Bayerische Bierhalle, a big, noisy place where beer was served in one-litre tankards, and a brass band played. My mother was there too (accompanying the cellist). She sat at the lower end of the table, at which Edwin sat at the head. He was already in full flow—the concert had been a scandal, more or less—and his piercing voice was telling one joke after another. Roars of laughter, while he remained serious. Open mouths, red cheeks. The leader of the orchestra looked thirty years younger and, when he got a word in, was telling stories about musicians.—At the lower end of the table, things were almost as lively. As my mother walked home on what was a mild, early summer's night, she was warbling away to herself, a Bartók melody that, during the concert, she'd thought she hadn't liked.

BACK then, it wasn't necessarily like my mother to warble away to herself. And Bartók, at that. That said, she no longer had her old manner either. She no longer stood, rigid, in the corners of rooms. She was no longer a child, of course, but an adult. One inclination had remained: her habit of clenching her fists and pressing them together so tightly that the blood shot to her brain. She would maintain this cerebral compression for a few moments, then let go again. No one ever saw this. It wasn't possible to see that, for a short time, she'd left the world. — She looked after her father, took care of the house. Did the shopping, supervised the maid, decided the seating plan when people were invited to dinner. Stepped in, when the guests arrived, for the woman of the house. Knew when to speak about the weather, and when to mention any honours, successes. She wore high-necked silk dresses that made her look a little teenager-like still. If she chatted to a guest — her father would be at the other end of the table — that guest would have her full attention, and yet not for a moment would she lose sight of the table. Raising her eyebrows barely noticeably, she would signal to the maid that the wine glass of one of the men was empty, or that one of the women had dropped her serviette. — But she had moments more often these days when she thought she'd burst into tears. Now, right now, this very second. But she never did cry, not ever. How much would she have liked to — though, or rather: *because* crying was the ultimate no-no. Her father never cried, of that she was sure. Her grandfather had certainly not cried, and her great-grandfather very definitely not. These strong men!—She often now stared into space, into some distance or other. At moments like this, she knew for sure she was as nothing, a nobody, like thin air or rather, to everyone's irritation, something excrement-like that someone should take a floor-cloth to.—When she did end up in a corner again, big and small at once, and clenching her fists, she was no longer in control, but subjugating herself. To whoever happened to be there, and for whatever reason. She would look deep inside, see herself in herself, as before. Now, though, she was kneeling at the feet of a king, or a murderer, who was wearing gigantic, long boots; her little self could see only the toes, the laces at most, the mud from walking, blood from the hunt. She would wipe them clean, these gigantic shoes, would wipe and clean them, lick them, then finally, humbly, look up, way up to the king's face hovering beneath the sun, and the beard that was hanging towards her. His eyes, such glowing coals! She knew instantly, while her head was still turned upwards and her gentle hands were wiping the shoes—yes, she *knew*!—that it was forbidden, completely forbidden, to see the sublime, and that her master had caught her in the act. Already, the shoes were kicking out, were kicking her in the face, or the abdomen. She remained silent, though, for in the presence of the king one didn't make a sound. Wretched but happy, she crawled into the very back of her cave.—Some sound or other would rouse her, and she'd find her way back. Hurry into the kitchen or the smoking room, wipe away some dust, and straighten a chair.—Her nights (she was still able to sleep at that point) were consumed by dark dreams. She got up every morning at six. Had to. Her father was an early riser and expected (anything else was, for him, unimaginable) her to make his breakfast. Just as his wife had done. As all women used to. And so she made coffee and warmed the bread while her father, at the table in the drawing room, read the morning paper. — In the summer this was doable, there was an early sun outside. But in winter! Her room was like ice. (Her father wouldn't countenance her stove burning overnight.) Her clothes were frozen stiff. Her pants crunched as she pulled them up. Her stockings crackled. — The whirling sensations she felt would threaten, at moments like this, to whip every last piece of her away. It was as if, somewhere deep inside, she could gurgle away, could fold in and completely vanish, sucked away by a deadly inner whirlpool. — A fright. A fear. Panic. — On days like that, she was extra precise. Instructed every muscle what to do. Completed every action very carefully. The fork now! And now the knife! — If, in the family recipe book, it said to use fifty grams of flour, she used fifty. Not forty-eight, not fifty-one. She'd rather have weighed the flour four times to check. She was a good cook. Her father praised her. 'Yes, yes, it tastes good, child.' Like at home, almost. — At home? She'd thought this was home.

MY mother was now at every concert of the Young Orchestra. Initially, she sat right at the back—the seats weren't numbered—near the local composer who always sat at the far end of the back row, beside the fire exit. Somehow, however, from concert to concert, she found herself sitting further forward, either by coincidence, or because a friend waved her up to where she was sitting. From the fifth concert onwards, she installed herself directly behind Edwin. At the centre of the second row. — Edwin, from behind, looked older than he was. A magician in the tail coat he was paying for in instalments, fifty francs after each concert. — The concerts continued to be exciting. The musicians, the children that they were, played like crazy. Their enthusiasm spread to the audience, hardly one of whom had ever heard of the composers being performed. My mother didn't know Bartók or Křenek or Busoni either. — There continued to be furious battles afterwards, of course. Stravinsky's Second Suite, for example — *his* name my mother did know — was booed by the back of the hall while the front — where, as before, the fiancées and fathers were seated, but also — more and more — those who had been bitten by this new music — went wild with enthusiasm. — After each concert, everyone sat together, as they'd done after the first, just no longer in the Bayerische Bierhalle as a brass band made a racket there they hadn't noticed that first time. They now congregated at the Weisses Kreuz, a smoky inn, where only the members of a students' society were a nuisance. Each time the young men stood to attention round their table suddenly, their tankards raised to their chests as they roared some vow or other. — My mother would still sit at the lower end of the table, and Edwin at the top. They never spoke to each other. Edwin didn't even nod

to her when everyone parted. But after the seventh or eighth
concert he suddenly sat down beside her and revealed that
she'd stood out for him from the very first evening. That he'd
made inquiries about her. And that his friends' assessment of
her was favourable. The fame of the Young Orchestra was
now radiating beyond the borders of the town, he told her; he
knew of people who travelled from Winterthur and Lenzburg
to hear them; all of this added up to organizational work that
was beyond him. He also wanted to introduce a subscription
series. In short, Edwin asked my mother, would she be
interested in being a maid-of-all-work, the heart and brain of
the Young Orchestra? Box office, preparation of the guest
performances that would now surely follow, looking after
the soloists, being there to comfort any Orchestra member
who might take ill or have problems. He looked at her, all
serious, and without even a moment's consideration, she said
yes. There was no talk of payment. No one in the Young
Orchestra was paid, not even Edwin. The only money was for
the composers, and that wasn't much either.

SHE threw herself into the work. There was so much to do!
Up until that point, just as an example, the money for all the
tickets they sold had ended up in a shoe box, and Edwin had
taken what he'd needed for the Orchestra. Now, my mother
opened an account at the Creditanstalt, and bought five
Leitz files that she labelled and put on a shelf. She looked at
them, and her heart beat harder. Revenue! Expenditure!

General Correspondence! Subscriptions! Advertising! Her handwriting was beautiful. Her bookkeeping, written with a sharp nib and Indian ink, was a work of art. One figure under another, the delicate lines above and below the totals like bars. The lines all drawn with a ruler, the final totals in red, and double-underlined. No blots anywhere.—She'd paid for the files with her own money, of course. She also paid for the paper, the postage, the printing of leaflets. She'd dared—she was now twenty-three, after all—to ask her father for pocket money every month. She'd stood there, on her side of the desk at which he sat, enthroned, her fists clenched, her chin red and pointing at him. She was trembling. Her father looked at her, his child. What was wrong? Didn't he feed her? Buy her clothes? Pay her dental bills? Then he saw the glow in her eyes. He nodded. 'Twenty francs,' he said. 'And I expect you to account for all of it!' He nodded again. My mother breathed out again and left.—She wrote letters to the soloists, beseeching them to play for free. She spelled out why they should: the music was so splendid, appearing with the Orchestra a boost for every career. Sometimes she even called them, using Papa's telephone that looked like a monster of some sort, and had a two-digit number. Her Papa didn't notice *everything*!—The soloists then lived at her place, in the two garrets beneath the roof. Her father, who encountered them sometimes at breakfast, was polite and offered them sugar and cream, though he preferred Puccini to Darius Milhaud, and continued to attend the concerts at the Phil-harmonic. Those of the Young Orchestra he ignored, the musicians at his breakfast table he considered to be children who had yet to learn about the pains of life and, indeed, music. He grew extremely fond, mind you, of one young bassoonist—young enough to be his son—to an extent that took the young man, my mother, and her father himself by surprise. He came from Bergamo, the bassoonist, and knew about preparing sauces in a way that not even her father did. My mother had fetched him from the station, or rather: had wanted to, for he'd got off the train on the wrong side, and she'd spotted him only once it had left again. Some distance away, he was already negotiating the tracks, up, down, further and further away. When he was down at the level of the tracks she could see only the tip of his bassoon, like a periscope, above the platform. Then he vanished between the houses. Couldn't be found all afternoon, and was less than sober when he turned up, in the evening, for the dress rehearsal. His performance at the concert, though, proved to be brilliant.—At their first breakfast together, my mother's father promptly fell so in love with this fellow Italian—his wife had been dead for six years now—that he attended his concert, clapped until his hands were sore, and the next morning invited him to stay. For a whole week, they cooked Italian dishes together—*ossobuco*, tripe and *riso trifolato*. Discussed things with flushed faces, and in Italian, always. As a farewell gift, my mother's father—a man so affected by his former poverty that even his late wife had considered him mean—bought his new friend a wickedly expensive contra-bassoon from Calinieri. As his friend made his way down the garden path, shouting 'Ciao' and 'Grazie per tutto', tears were pouring from my mother's father's eyes, tears that my mother, who was standing beside him, waving, failed to see, so convinced was she that her father never cried. The latter went on to write the bassoonist several letters, full of recipes, and hinting at his loneliness. Not a single reply did he receive. In the autumn, he drove his Fiat to Bergamo—this time over the Julier, Bernina and Aprica passes—and found at the address the bassoonist had given him a woman with three children who cried in anything but harmony. Talk about dissonance! And no bassoonist. A day later, he managed to find him after all, after a performance of Ernani at the Opera House. He was leaving by the stage door, arm-in-arm with a woman with black hair. 'Oreste!,' my mother's father shouted. 'Sono io! Ultimo!' But the bassoonist didn't recognize him, continued to chat to the woman. Ultimo watched them until they vanished round a corner. The next morning, he drove home.—Before each rehearsal, my mother would set out the chairs and music stands, in exactly the right positions. She checked that the room was heated properly. That no air was coming from any of the blowers. If, during the rehearsal, someone was speaking loudly somewhere in the building, or hammering even, she would dart out like a fury. There'd be immediate silence again, even if the director himself—they were still based in the Historical Museum—was the source of the noise. She was always the first to arrive, and the last to leave. She designed a logo for the posters and headed notepaper: the first letters of the orchestra's name, entwined. There was now also a chorus, and my mother ensured there was always enough tea at its rehearsals. Edwin didn't even notice that he no longer had to open doors for himself. That my mother did it for him as he approached each time, with a score—leafed through so often, it was in tatters—under his arm, and his eyes looking way ahead. How splendid he was! Bursting with energy, he'd jump on to the stage, look at all the musicians at once, then whip them into the heavens of the music. During the rehearsals, my mother would sit among the suits of armour, even seated she was taller than them, and always have paper and pencil in her lap. For sometimes, while continuing to conduct, Edwin would shout out 'Why is the trombone player's chair creaking?' or 'We need a biographical note on Schoeck for the programme, by tomorrow.' She would note these things right away, would replace the chair and, that same evening, would persuade the local composer, over half a litre of *dôle*, to tell her all he knew about Othmar Schoeck. Which, if not systematic, and not entirely accurate, was a lot. She wrote it all down, re-wrote it *at home*, re-wrote it again, then finally wrote it out neatly. Handed the manuscript to Edwin, who nodded, distracted, and crumpled it into his pocket. She only had eyes for him. She'd no idea that she glowed, that she devoured him with her eyes when he stood before the Orchestra, asking it to repeat bar 112 until the first violins were really rubbing *pianississimo* against the melodic arc of the oboes. (There were now oboes in the orchestra; as well as clarinets, horns, and trombones.) The musicians noticed my mother's eyes. Very much so. Only Edwin didn't.—

The press now attended the concerts, of late even Friedhelm Zust, *the* local music critic. He purchased a ticket without a grumble. It seemed to amuse him, even, that he had to pay. It didn't, in any case, influence his reviews, though he remained in the clutches of Beethoven and Tchaikovsky and couldn't see much in someone like Prokofiev. My mother cut out all the reviews and stuck them in an album. She was thrilled. She was happy.

HER father now permitted her — even he could see she was a grown woman — to go to balls organized by the parents of friends and acquaintances for their now grown-up daughters and sons. Not the families with the biggest names, it's true, but they all had money. The other deputy directors of the firm, for example, or doctor and lawyer friends. (The Bodmers, the Montmollins and the Lermitiers had different guest lists.) In winter, it was parties beneath a blaze of lights in salons, from which the oak tables and rugs had been removed. In summer, parties in town gardens full of Chinese lanterns. My mother no longer wore high-necked dresses but swept in swaying skirts across the dance floor. Low necks, bright colours, flowery patterns. A red rose at her breast, sometimes. She loved to dance, with unwavering seriousness, even when the others, merry from the champagne, were just hopping around; and had been for a while. She glided. Her shoulders were always level, indeed, if you'd placed a glass of champagne on them, not a drop would have spilled. Soon, the best dancers wanted to dance with her—with her, only with her. She happily took her lead from each, following that lead even as the man, himself, was discovering it. When one of the men, a Herr Hirsch—a German from Frankfurt, enrolled for two semesters at the local university—mistook the abandon with which she danced as passion for him and kissed her in a winter garden, she went stiff as a board. She had yet to give the matter any thought but, genuinely indignant, was able to tell Herr Hirsch, without hesitation, that she was keeping herself for the right person, and he was the wrong one. (She truly hadn't noticed that, without exception, her girlfriends were melting against their dance partners like wax in the sun; nor that they, in the same winter garden, or dark corners of the garden, were enjoying the hands that, in unambiguous fashion, slipped up their skirts. That their lips were giving as good as those that kissed them. She didn't think it possible in the case of girlfriends, women whom she knew, who were just like her.) She danced on, twirled and twirled.—In hot summers, the lawyers' daughters and deputy directors' sons went on excursions, across meadows and through forests, to secluded mountain lakes where they would swim in improvised swimming costumes—underpants, underskirts— that afterwards, back on shore, would cling to their bodies. The men, at times, swam naked even. It was the twenties, still the twenties, and no one was prudish, prudishness didn't exist. The men smiled, knowingly, as they recited poems in praise of opium. The women had bobs, smoked Egyptian cigarettes through long cigarette holders. My mother, too, swam in her underskirt, alongside her in the water, a stark naked Herr Hirsch. *That* was okay, *that* wasn't the problem. Still wet, and only half-dressed, they ate their picnic from baskets, laughing and joking loudly. My mother, a little to the side, smiling seriously. — Her father now let her borrow the car from time to time. Often, the whole gang was in it, piled one on top of the other, my mother at the wheel. They'd drive to a country inn in the foothills of the Alps, or right round the lake. Breaks at wooden tables, beneath vines; not one of them, not my mother, even, would be completely sober when evening came. The top of the Fiat would now be down and, shaking their heads, the farmers in the fields would watch the strange wagon-load vanishing into the setting sun. The police would just smile too. — No one, my mother least of all, would ever have thought of inviting Edwin. More and more often she came to rehearsals in the Fiat though, and would drive him home afterwards. He was still living in the industrial part of town. She'd drop him off at his door but keep the engine running. And drive straight off again.

THE first guest performance of the Young Orchestra was in Paris, if you don't mind. The 3èmes Journées de Musique Contemporaine were taking place there, you see, a series of events that presented the latest new music and had already made a name for itself with the French premiere of Rhapsody in Blue. My mother had to write and send telegram after telegram; finally, however, they were all on the train to Paris

—twenty-eight musicians, their conductor, and she herself.
Everyone had a packed lunch that my mother had prepared
the night before. A cheese sandwich and an apple. Raspberry
cordial to drink, from water-flasks. They were all in high
spirits and pointed out to each other the pools and ponds in
the light of the weak sun as the train raced past. Poplars,
weeping willows, colourful forests, here and there a distant
village, its grey houses. Flat as a pancake everywhere was,
between Basel and Paris-East. They arrived in the evening,
on the eve of the concert, looked for the hotel recommended
to my mother by the first double bassist, which she'd promptly
booked from top to bottom, and that turned out to be
even shabbier than, in her worst dreams, she'd imagined.
Damp walls, and flame-patterned wallpaper, a dismal blue or
Bordeaux-red, that was peeling from the walls. They were in
Paris, though, where misery was part of the folklore and
helped make the rest of the city seem even more beautiful.
They went for a walk, a procession of chattering girls
and boys, through the Quartier Latin, marvelled at Saint-
Germain-des Prés, and ate in a restaurant called À La Soupe
Chinoise. It was chop suey all round, a dish that no one knew
and cost three francs. To go with it, *un ballon de rouge*: Edwin,
a man of the world, knew what to ask for. Late, happy and
somewhat tipsy, they all fell into bed, and the hotel—had the
late revellers, still out and about, been attuned to it—shook
with the regular breathing of the thirty sleeping musicians,
their dreams all in major.—The next morning, my mother
took the Metro to the Mutualité and inspected the hall, alone.

34

It was a cavern without much light, with banners of the Syndicat des Transports Publics Parisiens all over the walls, but — beneath the lighting in the evening — had an exciting atmosphere. So she was assured, at least, by the person representing the organizer, a young man trying to look like Trotsky. My mother set out the chairs and music stands. The dress rehearsal was to the satisfaction of all concerned; so excited were they, they barely noticed that the heating wasn't working — it was only October, you'd have thought it was December, though — nor the fact the temperature in the hall wasn't even 12°C. It was hardly any warmer in the evening. Thirty-four people came, among them Maurice Ravel, a thin man in a heavy coat, who sat at the end of the third row, beside a young woman, the tip of whose nose, only, was visible among her furs. The Young Orchestra played Willy Burkhard's Lieder nach Tagore, Armand Hiebner's Sarabande for a String Orchestra and Continuo, and the Second Suite of the very Ravel sitting in the audience. Ravel came up at the end and shook Edwin's hand. *'Bien, très bien,'* he murmured. *'Continuez comme ça.'* That he didn't join them for supper did nothing to lessen the mood, and Edwin announced that all their food and drink was on the Orchestra. My mother blanched at this, initially, but then got more and more caught up in everyone's joy; at the end of the evening, she cheerfully paid an amount that made nonsense of the recently agreed annual budget. By two or three in the morning, they'd all eaten their fill, everyone was drunk, and the Orchestra bankrupt. Singing, they made their way along Boulevard Saint-Germain, their hotel was in one of the narrow side streets. Edwin had linked arms with my mother, who, like him, was singing loudly; and just as perfectly. The whole Orchestra was singing, polyphonic. It was popular songs they were singing, though, like 'Heut geh ich ins Maxim' or 'Ich wollt ich wär ein Huhn', rather than pieces from their repertoire. At the hotel—everyone was fooling around and hugging each other—Edwin ended up in my mother's room somehow and kissed her. She, of course, returned his kisses. He was the right person. He stayed the night, what remained of it, and in the grey light of morning they were still rolling and tumbling, laughing, in love, hugging and kissing, fulfilled, redeemed. It was wonderful. At seven in the morning, my mother got up—Edwin stayed where he was—as she'd to return to the Mutualité before they got their train. To finalize money matters, and collect the felt hat a viola player had forgotten. The young Trotsky was there again; he, too, bleary-eyed. My mother was given their percentage of the box office for thirty-two paying customers—little enough in itself—signed the receipt, and gave the revolutionary a goodbye kiss. Your man didn't know what was happening, and blushed deeply. My mother donned the viola player's hat, rushed to the Gare de l'Est, jumped into the last carriage, and squeezed in—since all the compartments were full—beside the cellist. Edwin was somewhere too, reading a score. They were all much quieter than on the way there. My mother slept too, her head on her friend's shoulder. She squinted, later, at the stretches of water with willows whizzing past. At cows, horses, at farmers watching the train and scratching their heads. It was night again when they got home. They parted without a great fuss. My mother walked home, straight across town. Her feet rustled in the leaves, and her heart was burning.

THE next morning her father died. It was barely six o'clock when my mother, still aglow with enthusiasm for what she'd just experienced, came running into the drawing room because, as she fiddled with the coffee pot in the kitchen, she'd heard a kind of cry, a gurgle for help, a snorting with rage. Ultimo was lying beside the potted palm, the Saturday paper crumpled in his right fist. It was terrible: he was staring up at my mother, his mouth wide open, his breathing coming and going, in bursts. My mother knew immediately he was dying. And indeed: Ultimo was lying there, silent and motionless, when the doctor — not even a quarter of an hour later — came rushing through the door. He knelt down beside him, anyway, sounded his heart and lungs, felt his pulse, and flashed a torch in his eyes. When he closed them for him, with two fingers of his right hand, my mother's lips started to tremble. Her chin and hands were shaking, her knees, too, so much so, she lowered herself onto a stool. Ultimo was lying there naked — his dressing-gown had opened — looking strange and angry. Thick lips, white hair, a wiry beard. Black skin. My mother's whole body was shaking, she'd to hold on to the mantlepiece when she got up to throw a blanket over him. The doctor cleared his throat and said, 'Yes, well, I have to go now,' and it was only at this point she noticed he'd just pulled a raincoat on over his blue-and-white striped pyjamas, and his bare feet were in slippers. 'Chin up, Miss!' He closed the door behind him, without turning back. My mother continued to tremble for another hour, then — unconsciously — set about organizing the funeral as if it were just another guest performance by the Orchestra. The obituary notices, the many *faire-part* — almost a hundred, with addresses in France, Italy, USA — the registry office, the parish. The undertaker's. She chose a coffin fit for a king although, or because, Ultimo would never have lain in such a thing. The funeral was in a cemetery, actually long since closed, up on what were once the town fortifications, the redoubts, in a garden full of ancient trees and Michaelmas daisies, from where the dead could see down onto the lake, and as far as the white mountains. Ultimo, when he got married, had acquired a family grave, with space for four bodies. His wife had been lying there for nine years. Now it was his turn. Fifty-five years later, his daughter, my mother, was buried by his side — and so, today, one space remains. The grave, just as back then, is between the palatial memorials of the Scheuchzer-Vom Moos and Ebmatinger families, and portrays — following his wife's death, Ultimo had ordered the statue from the same artist who created the Ebmatinger's marble mourners — a grief-stricken marble angel with giant wings, comforting, or crushing to death, a humble man with a hat and briefcase and a little girl, both of whom have flung themselves over the body of a woman. These two are made of a darker stone, and the girl looks very pregnant. — It was a glorious autumn day. The sky blue, like in a painting, the birds flying high. Half the town population—with the exception of the Bodmers, the Montmollins and the Lermitiers, naturally—was squeezed in between the weeping willows and the temples, the inscriptions on all of which highlighted the glory of special men and women, now deceased. There wasn't one who hadn't been a procurator or, at the very least, a philanthropist. Here and there, a child, its photo beneath glass, distressing. A priest spoke, flapping his wings like a bird, while my mother—all the time he sang his holy songs— was waiting for lightning to strike from the heavens to leave the priest and her in no doubt that Ultimo, even in death, wanted nothing to do with *this* god. That my mother—there was no will—had wantonly scorned his last requests. That *his* god was still a lion. But nothing happened. A friend from his young days made a pitiful attempt to recall the tricks they'd got up to as students, and finally, the main speaker, the director of the firm, spoke in praise of his colleague's work ethic. He closed with the suggestion that, without the dead man's input, the production of utility vehicles would not have reached the levels it had. That is to say, he wished, no doubt, to close with these or similar words, but was so overcome by a bad coughing fit that he gave up mid-sentence and, still coughing, went over to my mother and, *still* coughing, squeezed her hands.—Afterwards, they all went to a restaurant down by the lake—the director coughing and spluttering, still—to the posh hotel in town. Seated round white tables, they ate dried beef and dry-cured ham and drank wine from Ultimo's home region: Chianti, admittedly, not a Barolo; but all the same. — The atmosphere, nevertheless, wasn't what it might have been. On the contrary: even if this one or that one tried to entertain them all with a sad-but-wonderful memory, with each bite or gulp, they were all getting more irritable, more distraught, more appalled. One of them, the public prosecutor of the town's juvenile court, seemed to be out of his senses after barely two glasses, and was speaking loudly to himself. His neighbour, a partner in a private bank, went red and finally starting shouting at the public prosecutor, 'Do I have to listen to this? Do I? Must I?' — then burst into tears and ran to the loo. No one was able or wanted to check he was okay as Ultimo's chess partner of many years — a notary who had married a Lermitier, at least, albeit one from a collateral line — suddenly banged his fist on the table, hit his wine glass — which promptly smashed into pieces — and, waving his bleeding hand around, roared that this was their punishment, God's punishment, the Lord's punishment. Hadn't he always said it. Gone, gone, it was all gone, the future was gone. His blood sprayed all over the table and onto the cellist's blouse. She jumped up and stared, horrified, at the stains on her chest. — It was the bad tidings from Wall Street that got them all so worked up. There wasn't one of them who, over night, hadn't lost his entire fortune, or half of it, at least. Soon, they were all standing round the tables, shouting at each other, as if the person who successfully shouted down the other would get a last chance. The private banker was now back again, was the only one still sitting at his place, and was continuing to cry quietly. A woman, a lady with a mink stole round her neck and gold bangles on her arms, tried to push between two of the men throwing a fit — her husband and her lover — to calm them, and got such a hefty wallop in the face that she flew over a chair and under the table. It was hard to say who'd hit her, her husband or her lover. Maybe both. Both, anyway, stuttering their apologies, wanted to help her up again, she wouldn't accept their help, though, and screamed from under the table that they both had puny dicks. There was no difference between them, none at all. And yes, as she wanted everyone to hear, it was true: neither had ever satisfied her. Not a *single* once. — At that, she crawled out from under the table and ran off, her bangles jangling, her nose bleeding, the mink dragging behind her. — This was the signal for everyone else to make their exit too. They pushed and jostled to get through the narrow door and, sprinting past each other, fled out into the open. The racket they were making became more and more distant. Suddenly, there was a silence, like after an explosion. My mother was sitting alone at one of the tables, staring at glasses that had been knocked over, at broken glass, the wine stains, and blood. A fly that was buzzing around stopped, then started again. Finally, my mother sighed, stood up, and turned around. Along one wall, at a long table, motionless and silent, sat ten to twenty guests dressed in black, with red, no, black, actually, faces, forests of hair, and thick lips. A horde of giants, with paws rather than hands, the children too. My mother stared at the strange guests, and they looked back at her, their eyes wide open. For a long time, for several breaths, no one moved. Suddenly, though, the biggest of the monsters—a genuine forefather—stood up, went up to my mother, opened his arms, and shouted, '*Ma guarda un pò! Clara! La piccola Clara!*'—It was Ultimo's brothers, and the last of his sisters. Also: the sister's husband, the brothers' wives, the children and the grandchildren. And a few distant cousins, both male and female, and a few people of whom no one knew how and whether they were related to Ultimo. All of them, though they'd not ever visited the living Ultimo, wished to take leave of the dead one. '*Vieni, Chiarina, siediti!*' My mother sat down beside her uncle. Next thing, they were all speaking, and all at once. Even the children's voices sounded like rocks crashing down mountains. My mother tried to answer and was delighted to discover she could speak Italian. '*Cara zia! Carissimo zio!*' She began to prattle on, '*Ah, se sapessi, zio mio, la mia vita! Dolori! Lacrime! Un martirio!*', was soon getting braver and braver, adding a *magari* here and a *dunque* there. They'd all turned to her now and were listening to how she spoke. Oh, ah, this was her blood. She was starting to feel safer and safer among these mountain giants, more protected, felt herself getting smaller and smaller, and with their permission. Clara, *la piccola Clara*. When long after midnight they left the restaurant—the bill gobbled up all the money my mother still possessed—they were all laughing, and shouting over each other, they hugged each other once, and they hugged each other again, shouted, as they walked off, something else they'd remembered, one last joke for the road. Those who'd come along for the ride, for the pleasure of it, who didn't remember Ultimo, did exactly the same. My mother waved until the very last of her re-found family had vanished into an old-town lane — their laughter remained audible for a while — then went home, back to the empty house. She threw herself into bed, determined to sleep on, the next morning — longer than ever before. Until lunchtime, later! She'd promised her uncles and aunt, she'd come immediately, sooner than the day after next, in spring at the latest, to Villa di Domodossola, to see the stone dwelling where Ultimo's life had begun.

IN the weeks, months even, that followed, my mother was busy tidying up the house — she stood the potted palm that had been knocked over up again, and washed his last breakfast dishes; trying to understand and check the books in which her father had carefully noted all revenues and expenditures; finding and organizing his stocks and shares; finding out which banks her father had used; dealing with any death duties; speaking to the firm's director about the financial side of her father's death — his contract provided for no payments beyond his death; and attending to any unpaid bills. Her father had no debts, of course. He, who was so conscientious. That said, the new tyres for the Fiat had yet to be paid for, as had forty-eight bottles of Mouton Rothschild, ready to drink, from 1919. It was the first time her father had been disloyal to his home region. — The Orchestra, of course, came on top of that. The Mozart Days were taking place in town just then, and the Young Orchestra ventured into new territory by playing unknown pieces — unknown in the town, at least — such as K. 134, K. 320e and K. 611. Each and every one, a premiere. (Later, Edwin was to conduct *Idomeneo*, never before played in the town, the concerto version, with Lisa Della Casa, Ernst Haefliger and Paul Sandoz. But that was later, a great deal later, and was to be one of the Orchestra's greatest triumphs. Edwin had become a Mozart specialist in the interim. It's true he continued to exclude the pieces everyone loves. There was no Jupiter Symphony, no K. 491, no Marriage of Figaro Overture. Nor did he ever include the Symphony in G minor. By now, though, he loved this piece so much, he acquired the original score *before* he made his first billion. An incredible stroke of luck, a one-off opportunity, and a costly matter.) — My mother, then, was charging round, checking before the rehearsals was the heating working, or in any way noisy, straightening the seats, getting the tea ready, all that kind of thing. It was a hectic time, and could, almost, have been a nice time. A lot of hustle and bustle, a lot of applause, lots of new people. A young Rudolf Serkin played two early piano concertos, K. 175 and K. 246. My mother thought she was dreaming, blind but seeing, deaf but hearing, numb but feeling. — Once she'd looked through all the papers, spoken to all her father's banks, and — sitting at her father's desk — had added and re-added and re-added again, the shock she got was so sudden that her heart was palpitating and she jumped up and tore the window open. She was breathing heavily, inhaling the cold autumn air, and ten, or even twenty, deep breaths later, she *understood*. That she was poor now. Had no money at all, zilch, *niente*. She was twenty-four years old, had no qualifications, was beautiful, and had never been without money. In the account was nothing more than her father's final wage. The securities—Ford, Mechanical Irons, White Sewing Machine and other dead certs—had become worthless.—True, she still had the car and the house. But the Fiat wasn't exactly new any more, and she could be glad a friend of her father had given her one thousand and five hundred francs for it. It was even worse, in the case of the house. She soon realized that only a few property sharks were buying houses—prices having hit rock bottom—everyone else, just like her, had no money. There was a mortgage of a hundred and fifty thousand francs on the house, and one of the partners at Sarazin, Sarazin & Rochat offered her precisely that amount. A hundred and fifty thousand minus a hundred and fifty thousand was nothing. She gave the house away because she couldn't have paid the interest on it.—All this time, she'd barely seen Edwin. She didn't know why, ran into him two or three times at the office, at rehearsals, didn't otherwise. She'd so much to think of, she hardly ever thought of Edwin, not at all, actually. On one occasion, she'd dreamt of him or, maybe, her father. He was a big horse and kicking at her, without connecting, albeit. She ran off, as if harassed, nonetheless, slipped on a patch of ice, slid and slid and—still looking for something to grab onto—went crashing into a hole, the type Eskimos cut in the ice when they want to catch seals. She sank down into bright blue water. Far above, she could see Edwin looking down the hole in the ice at her. Sinking further, she reached up towards him. He didn't move. — She woke, shivering again. — On the day she gifted the house to Herr Sarazin, she came across Edwin in the office. He was flicking through the subscriptions and hardly said hello. She sat down at her desk and said, 'I need a room. A cheap one.'

Edwin raised his head and said, 'Mine is about to be vacant.'

'Your room?'

'I've worked it out. The town pays me quite well for Mozart. In addition to that, I've another five appearances as guest conductor before the end of the year. I've rented an apartment by the river. Three rooms, balcony looking onto the water. Very beautiful, you'll see.'

My mother gulped. She stared at the proof of a poster for the next concert. The letters were dancing. 'I'll take the room,' she said.

AND, suddenly, May had arrived, spring was blossoming before my mother could keep her promise to visit her uncles, her aunt and all her other relatives. That said, it was pouring with rain as she carried her small leather suitcase — an heirloom, covered with stickers from hotels like the Suvretta and the Danieli — to the station. She travelled third class. It poured as she changed trains in Berne, and a real deluge descended from the sky as she sat in the station buffet in Brig, waiting for her connection to Domodossola. That train, when it came, consisted of a tiny little steam engine, a trolley from which steam issued, rather, and two carriages of the Italian state railway which had a separate door for each compartment. The tickets were checked in the station as people boarded, that is, a ticket inspector watched, unmoved and dry, as the few passengers fought their way to the train through the celestial waterfalls. In the compartment, my soaking wet mother sat with a similarly soaked priest who, initially, pretended to read the Bible and soon, due to the heat (the air in the compartment was from the south) and his wet cassock, was just filling the place with steam. From my mother's clothes, too, rose a white haze. The train finally jerked into motion and disappeared into the tunnel. No light, just — for brief moments — the reflection of the rare lamps outside. When she came out at the other end, the sun was so bright, so dazzling, my mother thought her eyes were in flames. She climbed down onto the platform, a cloud, a blind cloud. She couldn't see anything, it's true, but she could feel the heat of the sun on her skin, she was breathing a new air, and she could hear a voice calling her name, somewhere in the shining brightness. 'Clara!' A falsetto voice, as if a tropical bird were calling her. Through the inferno of light she gradually recognized Uncle No. 2, a gnome in too large a jacket, hopping up and down behind the customs barriers. She flung herself into his arms. Her uncle was so small and slight, his face vanished between her breasts, his arms could barely reach round her. Even so, he hugged and squeezed her so tight, she thought she'd broken all her ribs. '*Ahi, zio! Piano, piano!*' Her little uncle let go, took a deep breath — his head was a dark red — then laughed, lifted her suitcase and, at an angle to the weight of the suitcase, and speaking over his shoulder, walked across to a brand new lorry, a Fiat, on the tarpaulin of which two lions were painted, on their rear legs, and with a bunch of grapes in their paws. Beneath the picture, in big red letters, were the words: VINI MOLINARI. *Finito i muli! Basta con questi carri!* My mother got in beside her uncle, who was sitting on a cushion and could barely get his arms round the wheel, and they rolled down an empty street, on which the only person, beneath a halo of steam, was the priest on his way to a church. — Her uncle talked and talked. Laughed and talked, non-stop. My mother didn't understand a word; told him so, even. But her uncle simply repeated the same sounds, this time louder. He laughed a second time too, booming this time. So my mother let him chat, just, and looked out the window. They were driving along — her uncle the only one getting his jokes — between poplars and groves of fruit trees, and tighter and tighter rock walls on both sides; and stopped, after just a few minutes, outside the stone dwelling that looked so much like the rocks round about that my mother didn't notice the door until her uncle pushed it open. This, then, was where Ultimo came from. Junk, bottles, crates, broken barrels, pickaxes, tin buckets, cobwebs, that my mother, standing in the entrance, looked at helplessly. No light, the air musty. There wasn't a patch of space to step into, and so, soon, my mother turned back to her uncle who, indeed, had been waiting, quiet and motionless, behind her. He immediately started talking again, though; dragged her over to a mound, covered in ivy, beneath a chestnut tree; and told her a story about it that was so funny he was soon cackling again. It was the Negro's grave, that much she understood. What was so funny about it, however, escaped her — though her uncle repeated the punchline three times, and ended up screaming it. The Negro had died making love, had fathered a child as he breathed his last: who wouldn't want to die like that? — Beside that grave was a second that her uncle pretended not to see. — The dwelling wasn't their ultimate goal, clearly — my mother had thought the whole clan was still living in it — but no, her little uncle now turned the lorry, and they drove back the way they'd come, downhill at first, and then into the plain. They drove and drove, on and on; between hills on either side, finally, with churches and castles on top: a large part of the way, in fact, that the Negro had once done on foot, if in the opposite direction. The same villages, in which dogs were still barking! Cornfields, similar to those the doomed man had fought his way through! The vineyards! Here and there, there were even still ox carts. A veritable pilgrimage, it was. — After about two hours, in which her uncle hadn't stopped talking for a single second, they turned off the road so suddenly, so surprisingly, that my mother got a fright and screamed; they were about to crash, she thought, into the impenetrable thicket of brambles and tree-trunks before her. There was a gap, after all, though; cart-tracks amidst the undergrowth. Branches of trees scratched the bodywork on both sides. Leaves on the windscreen, lianas, meant they could hardly see. Next, though, they were making their way through a portal of white rock, Roman ruins with a great many columns, among which bushes were growing wildly; then floating—the engine was no longer audible—through roses, hyacinths, larkspur, oleander and bougainvillea. A big blue sky now. Ponds covered in water lilies. Dragonflies were humming, butterflies fluttering. Birds—birds were singing everywhere, orioles even, and goldfinches! Air—air like on the first day of Creation. They ended up outside a large house with countless windows, a palace,—a monastery from the old days, rather, for part of the building was a church with an impressive tower. Instantly, those monsters with fuzzy hair, thick lips and burned-leather skin rushed out of all the doors: her aunt, Uncle No. 3, her uncles' wives, her cousins, male and female, the children, the children's children, and all those who had come to Ultimo's funeral without knowing whether or not they were related. They were throwing their hats into the air too, just like the servants who were dancing wildly, and seemed to be even more pleased than their masters. My mother was hugged and kissed, several times by each of them. Suddenly, though—my mother, her head spinning now, was standing on the gravel, using her case to steady herself—they all fell silent. No one moved. Was that music, booming, she heard? A path opened up in the crowd, in any case, and her big uncle came marching down it, powerful, radiant, his arms, again, wide open. '*Willkommen*!' he said—in German! He lifted my mother, together with her case, until she was wriggling in the air above him—which had everyone roaring again—

and he put her down only when she begged him. — This was happiness! Oh yes, wonderful it was! — Compliant now — having abandoned herself—with no will of her own, my mother let her big uncle drag her into the house. She was given a room that had once been a monk's cell. No crucifix, though, not anywhere. Instead: a bed, a wash-stand with an old porcelain jug, a wardrobe, a bedside table with a candle on it. Out the window, the sky was aglow with the sun that was just sinking into distant vineyards. Swallows were darting to and fro. Crickets were chirping. A cat was in among the oleander, bathed in flame-like light. — Later, twenty of them, for sure, men and women, all sat at a long table in the kitchen, in a large vault full of pots and pans. Oil lamps lit their faces, in which their eyes and teeth shone brightly. Her family! My mother, of course, was sitting beside her big uncle who kept filling her plate up as if she were dying of starvation. On the other side of her sat her big uncle's wife. She was, like him, huge, but slim, almost too thin. She was dressed entirely in black, though they were all very much alive, and when she spoke, her *r*'s were that rare scratching *r*, *quella erre lombarda*, that humbles even kings from faraway regions, reminding them, as it does, how much power and culture they lack still. Opposite her sat Uncle No. 3, who reminded her a little of a carp as he was constantly opening and closing his mouth. Her aunt and her two little uncles' wives were doing the cooking. Flames flared up when they opened the flaps of the oven, or used a metal hook to remove a ring. Their shadows moved like giants on the walls. The food tasted wonderful, and the wine her big uncle was pouring from bulbous bottles without a label was delicious too. Everyone was talking and laughing, my mother too. — Much later, approaching midnight already, the door opened and a young man rushed in. He was sun-tanned and had an ice pick in one hand, a bunch of alpine roses in the other. Everyone said hello at once, there was laughter and shouting. 'Boris!' her big uncle shouted, jumping up so violently his chair fell over. 'Your mother was getting worried!' — Boris was his son. That very day he'd been climbing the Cima Bianca by a new route. Demolishing a plateful of polenta and ragout, he reported, radiant, his adventures. Falling stones, icefalls, a sudden change in the weather when he was in the middle of the wall! They were all hanging on his every word. 'Boris!' That was his mother. 'Come *sei bravo*!' — Boris was called Boris because her big uncle had once had a weakness for everything Russian. Perhaps because of the magnanimous Czar Nicholas; more likely, though, because he'd just got to know a young woman from St Petersburg who was working in the kitchen of Hotel Victoria and had recently fled from the thugs of the last ruler of all the Russians. — Boris was a *beau ténébreux* and, right away, looked deep into my mother's eyes. She returned his gaze. He gave her the roses and promised to take her to the Cima Bianca soon. By the normal route, he said, and smiled. It was the type of thing the two of them could do before breakfast. — Well into the night, my mother, carrying a candle, felt her way to the monk's cell, where she sank into her bed as if into a dream.

HER big uncle was speaking—was the only person speaking—in a quiet voice. But everyone was listening to what he said. He was the law. His brothers, her little uncles, seemed to be happy not to have to make any decisions. They would grin to themselves, do this, do that, do nothing. At least not what her big uncle did, who at six in the morning would head out to the vines, and at ten at night would still be bent over the accounts. He'd the details of all their revenues, all their expenditures, all their outstanding debts in his head; you could ask him at any time. The last thing he did before going to bed would be to write up the work plans for the next day—vineyard, store, cellar—and he'd hang them on the board. He kept an eye on everything: whether the barn door was locked and the vineyard lift oiled.—The women ruled the roost in their own way.—He was known to laugh now and then, very much so, would joke with the workers, but couldn't stand others—her little uncles, especially—preferring to work less. 'Fixed costs of one hundred thousand lire,' he said more than once to her two uncles. 'Do you think they come in on their own?' Told off, her uncles nodded and slipped into the kitchen where they permitted themselves a grappa.—Outside the house, automobiles, and not mules any more, now stood. The lorry, of course; a Skoda that had to cope with whatever came along—had transported a pig once, even, on the back seat; and an olive-green Jaguar with a triad horn that only her big uncle used. It was a right-hand drive, as it came from England. It was the only Jaguar in the whole of Italy. Its engine hummed barely audibly, and her big uncle drove it in a manner typical of its country of origin. — Year in, year out, he'd accompanied his father, the mule driver, as he drove the mules over the pass. His father at the head of the trek, behind the foremost carthorse, he himself at the rear. In the summer, with his tongue hanging out with thirst; in the winter, bent against the icy snow that blasted into his face. (Her little uncles had given up and stayed at home.) Even with just the two of them, on good days they'd led a dozen mules over the mountain, carrying three tons and more per journey, wine mainly, but also fruits, olive oil, or — not that they earned much profit — truffles from Alba. They were paid in accordance with a scale that wasn't written down anywhere, but was known to everyone, that took the gross weight, the length of the journey and the weather into consideration. When the Simplon Tunnel opened, in 1905, from one day to the next there was nothing to be transported. Ten minutes it now took for the wine casks to be driven through the mountain. All the mule drivers in the valley went out of business, all except my mother's father's father. Every morning, he set off as if nothing had happened. And always her big uncle accompanied him. Unlike the mule driver, he saw, from the rear, that each day fewer animals were ahead of him. Soon, they were out with a single mule, one final sleigh, and no goods. (Once in a while there were a few milk churns or a cask of wine for the hospice.) Her big uncle, as he took each step, was staring at the back of the mule driver, and calculating. Calculating one way, calculating another. Weighing the effort against the gain, again and again. Every time it worked out as a loss, every time. And so — they were

almost at the top of the pass at the time, and a storm was
blowing snow into their faces—he went up to the front and
roared the result of his calculations into his father's ears, that
is it would be cheaper to stay at home. The mule driver neither
stopped nor turned round, he shouted into the wind, 'My
father walked behind gnus and buffalo until they died. I'll
walk behind mules until I die.'—They continued in silence
until Brig.—On the return journey, at the same spot, almost,
the mule driver turned to his son, looked at him, and dropped
dead in the snow.—He was buried beside the Negro, and soon
the mounds above the graves looked so similar that no one
knew any more who was buried where.—Her big uncle found
a cigar-box full of banknotes behind the firewood. Italian lire
and Swiss francs, in large and small denominations, coins, all
mixed up. Some German banknotes too, Reichsmark, and a
Swedish ten-öre note. We're not talking a small amount; a lot
of money, it was. Her big uncle pocketed this inheritance and
used it to buy a wine-growing estate in Piedmont, between
Alba and Asti, pretty much. Five hectares, maybe six, with
vines that were now too old, the weeds rampant among them.
It produced barely ten thousand bottles a year, the content of
which the locals considered undrinkable, and could be sold
only with difficulty, even in the north. The estate was called—
of all things!—'I Cani' and had two dogs in its coat of arms,
on their hind legs, holding a bunch of grapes. The house had
once been a monastery, consecrated to Saint Domenicus. The
best wine from the estate—not a good wine, the best wasn't
good either—was called San Domenico in his honour. For her

big uncle, though, — and for all the others — the name was in honour of the mule driver, of course. The first thing her uncle did was doctor the coat of arms, turning the two dogs into lions. 'I Cani' became 'I Leoni'. The gods of the Negro's foes had remained his foes; the lions, he hoped, would protect him. He planted new vines, gave unknown varieties a try, tore all the weeds out, and sprayed so much blue vitriol that his land shone blue like no other. He spent days in the lab, blending his wines, was the first person in Piedmont to do so, diluting being a deadly sin there. His wines, though, were getting better and better, with the result that he was able to buy more land, and was soon producing forty thousand bottles from twelve hectares. Others now dealt with the transportation. But he still had many customers on the other side of the Alps. In Brig and Sion, his wines were drunk in one restaurant in every two, almost. He supplied the San Domenico — which was now really good — to as far away as Berne and Basel. I Leoni had a turnover in the millions, which impressed my mother even more when her uncle quoted the figure in lire. While the others were working, she — my mother — walked through the vineyards with her parasol, among the flowers, beneath the fig trees, in the shade of the vaults. She sat in the kitchen, thinking this and that, and even climbed up the tower once, she could almost see as far as the sea from it. She thought, fleetingly, she'd like to do that too: graft away, sweating, in the vineyards, until she fainted. — She was dreaming away to herself. Far below, the Jaguar pulled up. Her uncle got out, looking small. She called but he didn't look up.

Walking quickly, he entered the house. She closed her eyes, felt dizzy. — Life, she thought, was beautiful, yes. It was only when her manner got the better of her, really, that it was not.

HER manner. This puzzle, deep within her, that seemed strange to her too. Her manner, meanwhile, you see, was such that her whole body — but when? And why? — would become hot, her head, her heart, her stomach. A sudden heat would flood through her, as if, deep within, all the protective walls had collapsed at once, releasing a lethal lava that had long been bubbling there. As the heat flooded over her, she would clutch at the backs of chairs, or the edges of tables, to avoid being swept away. To remain alive. Her hands, though burning too, would turn white with the effort. To save herself, she would bite her lips and slap herself on the head. After — what, minutes? Hours? — the glowing hot terror would gurgle away, deep inside. She would cool down, begin to breathe more calmly, or to breathe at all. Her heart would begin to beat again. She would wash her face. Then look around. This time, she was still in her cell. There was the table with the blue oilcloth on it. The washbowl. The toothbrush beaker. Her suitcase in the corner. The bedside table with the candle. The bed. The ochre-coloured cupboard with the paint flaking off. The page of a calendar showing a shepherd with a dog. — Still trembling, my mother felt her way downstairs, to outside the house where her cousins were playing bocce. Were talking loudly, laughing loudly, where they waved to her. She tried to smile back. The sun was shining. Behind her, one bowl hammered against another, and her cousins howled.

ONCE she was back in the town, she slept with Edwin again. He made love differently now, different from in Paris. He gave orders. He turned up unexpectedly in the room that, until recently, had been his, where my mother now lived. He'd be standing there suddenly, would smile, stub his cigarette out on the bedside table and bark at my mother to get on the bed. He now knew how he wanted to make love, and my mother made love to him the way he wanted. She enjoyed it, though; it wasn't as if she didn't like him being strong, stern. He rarely stayed long, never really. He'd put his trousers back on and leave, thin-lipped, without a word. My mother would then stand there, somewhat confused, in her little den, looking at the bed, at the milk tumbler or the vermouth glass, the contents of which Edwin had downed in a oner before undoing his belt. She would go into the bathroom, wash herself at the bidet, look at herself in the mirror, attempt a smile, finally slip into her dress, her stockings, her shoes. She would also smoke a cigarette and look out the window, down into a courtyard where children were playing. — My mother was never in Edwin's new apartment beside the river. Not ever. He came to her, always. — As before, she worked for the Young Orchestra, subscriptions for which were now in such demand that the regulars filled all the seats in the Historical Museum. Edwin and my mother decided to make the dress rehearsal public, at reduced prices; the hall, for those performances too, was immediately full. — By now, so much money was coming in that Edwin could pay my mother a salary. Not a lot, but it covered her rent and everyday needs. The soloists now also received a fee of a sort, and the composers commissions of some sort. The musicians in the Orchestra, however, were still playing without being paid — the enthusiastic response was their reward — and Edwin also conducted for free. He earned his money — he was twenty-six now and no longer unknown in the profession — with appearances in Winterthur, in Geneva, in Munich. In Bordeaux, he had four fixed engagements each year, with their Orchestre Symphonique, where he took on even Beethoven and Mendelssohn. Once, he even stood in for someone at the opera in Stuttgart. *Pelléas et Mélisande.* No one had a clue how he could know the score so well that, having received the telephone call for help, he could simply get on the train and, three hours later, be in the orchestra pit. When he took his bow at the end, even the soloists were applauding. Only he looked gloomy. — He now had a friend, whose name was Werner, and who was called Wern by Edwin; by my mother, subsequently, too. Wern looked like a globe, a globe that was red in the face, and the face almost always had a cigar in it. He often only sucked the cigar, sucked it until it was so soft, it would fall apart when he did then want to light it. He was a chemist and had developed a substance that destroyed greenfly without also killing the plant. His invention was so successful that his employer —

Chemie Schlieren—doubled its turnover within a matter of months. He was spending less and less time in the lab, and more and more travelling: to Italy, initially; later to Spain; once even to Morocco. Wherever he went, he demonstrated his magic potion. Often, he was on the road for weeks. When he was in town, though, he and Edwin were inseparable. They would sit in the Baobab, a smoky inn by the river, talking. Drinking and smoking or, to be more precise, Wern was drinking and smoking. Edwin remained sober and yet got more and more intoxicated. My mother came too, occasionally, and sat beside Edwin, who hardly noticed her. But there she sat, his beloved, after all, drinking, smoking and silent. She would look at Edwin seriously and smile when Wern laughed. Now and then, she'd say something too, but Edwin—Wern likewise—was deaf to women's voices. These high frequencies, the vibrations of which told them something trivial was being uttered. Why should they focus on that?—And yet my mother had something important to say, and when Wern, at one point, went to the loo, she said it—that is, she was pregnant. She wanted to be pleased, didn't know whether she was permitted to be. Whether Edwin, the father, would also feel able to be pleased. Edwin's expression, indeed, hardened—he was not at all pleased—when, finally, he understood what my mother was saying. 'Pregnant?' he hissed. 'Since when?' He took Wern's glass and drank what was left in it.—Wern, too, who had returned from the loo, and from whom no secrets were kept, shared Edwin's view that a child in this world, right here, and at this moment, was a misfortune.

It would destroy my mother's life, and Edwin's, in any case.
Even the cellist, who happened to join them, — Edwin with his
jaws clenched, Wern red in the face and my mother staring at
her knees—put her arm round my mother and said, 'Don't
keep it, Clara. It'll be better that way, believe me.'—And so, a
few days later, and accompanied by the cellist, my mother went
to see a doctor by the rose garden, right beside the lake. Edwin
had set the appointment up. In the evening, it was, after seven.
The doctor was alone. No assistants. He was very polite, very
proper, asked my mother to sit on the examination chair. The
cellist held my mother's hand. Afterwards, they travelled home,
back to the room that had previously been Edwin's, where the
child that had just been killed had been conceived. The cellist
helped my mother into bed, kissed her and said to call if she
needed help. Even in the middle of the night. 'Promise?' My
mother nodded though she didn't have a telephone. For an
hour, two hours, she stared at the ceiling and then fell asleep. —
Wern knew a lot about music; in many areas, more than
Edwin. (He was self-taught and had perfect pitch.) He was
mad about folk music. Not necessarily the Swiss variety,
though five-franc pieces spinning round in soup bowls and the
alpenhorn certainly interested him. No, he was more interested
in more distant forms, Spanish, Arabic or Balkan. A female
voice from Bulgaria could leave him delirious. He often came
to the rehearsals, was the only outsider allowed to. Afterwards,
Edwin would ask his friend how *he* would handle the
beginning of the adagio. More slowly, even more slowly?
Edwin, he who didn't ever seek advice!—But they didn't just

speak about music. More and more frequently, it was the misery facing the masses that occupied their thoughts, and the notion that the dictatorship of the proletariat was the only possible way to transform the general unhappiness into happiness. It may have been Wern who raised the subject, but Edwin was soon at least as passionate. Often, they both spoke at the same time, Edwin red, and Wern almost blue in the face, their voices raised so much that the other customers fell silent and listened. My mother—back at the table, as if nothing had happened—was hearing, for the first time in her life, the names of Marx, Engels, Lenin, Trotsky. Stalin! Once, or every evening once again, Edwin shouted at his friend—as if it was *he* who was to be blamed for the wretchedness of the oppressed—that only equality for all could put an end to the current injustice. He was standing now, snorting, and boring his index finger into Wern's chest. Did he, Wern, realize— Wern nodded—that even here in this country, in so-called democratic Switzerland, not even five per cent of the population owned sixty per cent of the national wealth? Wern nodded again. And was that right? Wern continued to nod then shook his head. Had he forgotten—Edwin pulled Wern up to face him, and the unlit cigar fell from the latter's mouth— how, at the time of the general strike, the ruling class had had hired thugs from the militia fire at comrades who were fighting for their rights? That people had been killed, killed!— He let Wern go, snorted again and sat down. The customers in the inn applauded. Wern laughed, picked the cigar up, sat down again, too. My mother had remained seated.—Often, before closing time, they moved on to the Ticino, an inn behind the station, for a final red wine. Edwin now took some, also. Sometimes the other customers, not entirely sober either, all sang the 'Internationale' together, on their feet, men and women both, urging a better future on, radiant. Their eyes! — My mother would stand up, too, and sing. Holding her neighbours' hands. Her heart was beating. She hardly ever thought now of the child that had vanished; never actually. — The landlord sang the loudest.

SOME time later Béla Bartók paid his first visit to the town. Edwin, who in his very first concert had played the Suite op. 4, and who viewed the allegro barbaro as the key new composition of their epoch, had written to him in Budapest in the vague hope of getting a new piece of work from him; a world premiere, ideally. By return, almost, came not just a splendid piece — the second piano concerto — but Béla Bartók himself, and his wife. He wanted to play his concerto himself! My mother was at the station, as ever, but this time Edwin was there too, mooching up and down the platform, excitedly. Finally, the train from Budapest arrived, hardly more than an hour late. A good dozen sleepy passengers got out, with mountains of cases, on which the porters pounced. My mother, Edwin too, had expected a colossus, someone with gigantic strength and power. But Bartók was a slight little man they could almost have overlooked, and didn't overlook only because his wife, an energetic person, addressed Edwin.

'Ädwin?' Edwin, though it wasn't like him, was so out of his mind with excitement, he stuttered and forgot to introduce my mother. So she just trotted along behind them.—She had booked the Bartóks into the Hotel Zum Schwert, something the Young Orchestra had yet to stretch to for any composer or soloist. A wonderful room with a huge bed and Louis Quinze furniture. Bartók, though, had a headache and didn't look out the window at the lake and the peaks of the Alps, glistening in the distance.—At the first rehearsal, Edwin trembled a little, initially—with Bartók at the piano, as attentive as any pupil—but soon pulled himself together. Bartók played his part without a word. Just once, he got up quickly and stood beside Edwin and sang two or three bars. He conducted with both hands as he did. Then the orchestra played the section again, and it sounded as if the sky were opening.—At the concert, Bartók wore tails, somehow old-fashioned. He played wonderfully, and the orchestra had never been so good. At the end, incredible cheering erupted at the front of the hall; but the back of the hall took up the gauntlet and booed and whistled with equal passion. Bartók bowed, bowed again, and again, and laughed. Edwin smiled, too, for a few seconds. Bartók shook the hand of first the conductor, then all the musicians he could reach; in some cases, several times. He bowed again, finally opening his arms as if to embrace his audience. Flowers, my mother had thought of flowers too! She was beaming all over, her face deep red as she stood behind the little door, through which the artists went onto the stage. She felt this, the greatest concert in the history of the Young Orchestra, was her triumph; *her* triumph, a little, too. (Further back, they were whistling, still, on their keys.) She was confused, touched, shattered. — Bartók and his wife stayed longer than planned; almost a week in the end. They liked it in the Hotel Zum Schwert and in the town, even though Bartók, the morning after the concert already, felt less satisfied with himself and with his work, and told Edwin he would re-write the beginning of the second movement. Edwin protested at first, then nodded. — My mother had calculated that there would be no money for the next concert if the Bartóks stayed until the Sunday. They stayed, of course, until the Sunday. And it was then my mother who implored them to add on the Monday and the Tuesday. (For the next concert — which was a novelty and a great success — Edwin, in fact, programmed early Baroque music. Palestrina, Gabrieli, Bassani, Rhau and Frescobaldi. No soloists and no composers expecting a percentage.) — My mother showed Béla and Ditta — they were now on first-name terms! — the town's attractions: both cathedrals, the Grossmünster and the Kleinmünster, the redoubts, the guild houses. Soon, however, it was Bartók who was explaining to *her* what they were visiting together. Why Charlemagne, who sat, in stone, in the crypt of the Grossmünster, had such an impressive beard (because he'd once been the equivalent of God the Father for people), or — when they were marvelling at the house in which he was born — how the now-revered reformer died (the orthodox back then first quartered him, then burned him to death.) —

Edwin was with them again when Bartók and his wife boarded the train back to Budapest. By now, it was Wednesday. Bartók shook Edwin's hand and kissed Clara; his wife did the reverse. Edwin and my mother waved until they could no longer see the Bartóks' handkerchiefs in the distance, through the thick smoke of the railway engine. A final whistle, far off, and that was that. Edwin was so lost in thought as he walked alongside my mother, he didn't say cheerio when he turned into the street where he lived. My mother continued, straight ahead. Bartók, she loved his music. For days afterwards, she could still hear in her head the part where the piano sings over the strings as if it would like to learn to fly.

IT was then not Edwin, but Wern, who asked my mother to accompany him on a trip to Frankfurt. He didn't want to travel alone, in Germany, at a time like this. His expenses would cover her too, that wasn't a problem. My mother hesitated, initially; then really wanted to; finally, she asked Edwin. He nodded, without listening properly, was busy with something else. 'Go, just go.' And so they went to Frankfurt, where they stayed in the Frankfurter Hof. 'Good products,' Wern said, as my mother looked around, amazed, at Reception, 'Need a good hotel if you want to sell well.' They were given two adjacent rooms, with a connecting door they never used. Wern went about his business (he hoped to negotiate a licence with Chemische Werke in Höchst) and my mother wandered through the town. The sun was shining. There was a mild wind. Plane trees, with birds chirping in them, offered shade. Cars, a few horses still, too. The people looked cheerful; children, shrieking with joy, hitting out at each other. Lovers. Here and there, men in brown uniforms and red armbands. Flags everywhere. They were flapping in a wind that was blowing more now. A broad avenue. Flag cloth flapping wherever you looked, which seemed funny. At one point, a troop of policemen shot past, in step. A man beside her raised his arm, suddenly, and roared something she didn't catch. Others were shouting too, it sounded as if they were barking, she didn't like it much. But apart from that! She felt light. Further on, later, a commotion. Glass tinkling and people running. A woman, invisible, screamed. My mother was right beside a policeman with an alsatian dog on a lead. He was observing the scene. She looked at him, inquiringly. He, however, had no reason, manifestly, to intervene, and so my mother kept on walking. She liked the town, especially the countless streets, full of nooks and crannies, around the cathedral. The shops, the tradesmen. She saw a cobbler with such a long beard that it kept getting between his hammer and the sole of the boot he was working on. A goldsmith was bent over a ring, his magnifying glass up at one eye. A barber with round metal-rimmed glasses was soaping his client's hair in a shop so small that he himself was out in the street. Greengrocers, potters, junk dealers. And again and again, old men: their black cloaks, black hats, long beards and plaited hair. They spoke with their hands — really! — My mother turned

away so they couldn't see how much they made her laugh. —
She stood on the Römerberg square, admiring the splendour
of the Middle Ages. On the banks of the Main, she drank a
cider and then crossed the Iron Footbridge—below her, the
pleasure boats, the families waving from them—to get to the
Museum where she looked for a long time at a little garden, a
paradise. It was as if it wouldn't let her go. A naked Adam
and a naked Eve she liked, though, too. The most delicate of
veils over the woman's nakedness, see-through, wonderful. —
The student from Frankfurt came back to her, who had once
kissed her, and with whom she'd swum, he completely naked,
she in her underskirt which didn't cover her up any better
than Cranach's veil did Eve. She was no longer sure what the
student's name was. Something to do with game. When the
name came to her—Hirsch, as in *deer*—she laughed out loud.
Hirsch, exactly! Sami Hirsch. The man at Reception helped
her find the telephone number. Sami Hirsch was pleased,
invited her round for a glass of wine.—In the evening, Wern
was pensive, dejected even. Was business going badly? Wern
shook his head. They were sitting in the almost empty dining
room of the hotel, eating boiled beef with savoy cabbage. The
sweet was Rote Grütze, a red fruit jelly. It tasted better than
it sounded. The wine, however, was like sugared water. —My
mother asked Wern to go with her to see Sami—who hadn't
been the right person, but wished he had. They went on foot;
the street they needed, Bockenheimer Landstrasse, started
right behind the Opera. An unlit villa in a pitch-dark garden
the size of a park, right in the middle of town too. They felt

their way along a gravel path, finally found a bell, and rang it. The door opened almost immediately, still no light, and a woman, scurrying, and with a candle, led them through dim corridors, round a corner on the right, up a few stairs on the left, then up and down, and this way, then that, until they reached a large, high-ceilinged room, in which, at last, a light was burning. Electric light, concealed in chandeliers. Curtains in all the windows, the shutters barricaded. Sami Hirsch, now sporting a little moustache, came up to my mother, shook her hand. Welcomed Wern. Then he introduced his mother and his father, two dainty, old people with refined smiles. They sat down, drank wine, a very good one this time. Yes, Sami was well, he was healthy. He'd excellent memories of his time abroad. The dancing! Did she remember the time they swam together? — My mother chortled with pleasure. She told them how nice her afternoon had been, how funny. — The parents smiled, sipped at their glasses, but didn't say a word. The room was like a royal chamber, had a ceiling fresco, from which fluttery angels laughed down from behind clouds, and yet it also looked a little like a junk room. A storeroom. True, they were sitting on golden chairs around a precious table, but round about were piled sofas, armchairs, a *recamière*. Pictures, turned to face the wall, mostly, but also a large Leda whom the swan was licking between the legs. 'Are you moving house?' my mother asked her friend. 'I am — today,' he said. 'But my parents don't want to.' For the first time, the woman opened her mouth. 'You can't teach an old dog new tricks,' she said, so delicately that my mother leaned towards her. 'You let them pass away.' She put a hand on the arm of her husband, who was trembling. My mother looked to and fro, between them and Sami. The latter was no longer smiling. He was red in the face. Wern seemed agitated too, he opened his mouth to speak, then closed it again. My mother didn't quite understand; she became serious too, had a drink. Soon after that, they left, walked without a word through Frankfurt by night, back to the hotel. — In the train, on the journey home, my mother rediscovered her ease. That cheerfulness she wanted to retain for as long as she could. And so she was more than surprised when — they were crossing the bridge over the Rhine in Basel at the time — Wern jumped up and shouted, 'It would make you want to throw up! Make you want to throw up, it would!'

'What?' my mother said. 'Haven't we just had a lovely trip?'

Werner sat down again. 'That's it,' he said, much more quietly, more to himself. 'It's over.'

My mother looked at him with big eyes. Yes. It was over. That was it. But the trip had been lovely, which is what she then told Edwin.

THEN Edwin got married. Everyone seemed to have known about the wedding, absolutely everyone, for weeks. For my mother, who heard in passing, and days after the event —

'Where were *you* hiding? It was *splendid*!'—it was as if she'd been struck by lightning. She sat on a chair, rigid, blind, turned to stone in a world that was spinning round her; her breath taken away, perhaps; no tears, for sure. Screams deep inside, a burning heat and ice. Edwin's wife was the sole heir of the firm. Her father, the third generation to own the business, had died of a stroke, and Edwin had comforted her. She was a beauty. She flowed from her car, a Maybach with whitewall tyres, like running gold and silver. A flawless face with big lips, shining teeth, almond eyes. Big hats in summer. In winter, furs. Edwin moved into the estate above the lake, where he now resided among the old and modern masters. His wife loved paintings—Vermeer was her favourite, and she really did have one—and collected contemporary painters with bold intelligence. She owned more Picassos and Matisses than all the Swiss museums put together, and their best works at that. But also Swiss masters: Gubler, Auber-jonois, Vallotton, Camenisch.—Edwin, in all this splendour, blossomed. Laughing, he and his wife chased each other through the suite of rooms until she surrendered to him in the winter garden. They rolled among the orchids and knocked palms over. The servants, tactfully, closed their eyes.—Edwin hadn't said a word to my mother beforehand; somehow, the opportunity had never arisen. Then it was too late, anyhow. When her birthday then soon came along, someone from Fleurop delivered an orchid, a miracle of nature, wrapped in a large box, and with a small card, on which Edwin had written, in purple ink, 'All the best! E.'—A similar orchid, with a similar card, was to reach my mother for the next thirty-two years, always on her birthday, always an orchid, always purple ink. Then — my mother had turned sixty-one — the orchids stopped. Never again did one arrive, though she lived for another twenty-one years, and Edwin far longer. My mother wondered why Edwin's birthday greetings suddenly stopped, but didn't find an answer. — A few months later, she married too. She handed in her notice — in the weeks between his and her wedding, Edwin hadn't come to the office, at least not while she was there — and moved to a house at the edge of town, which was in the middle of cornfields, even if her house *just* counted as part of the town. There was a forest beyond the meadows. She had a large, wild garden that, with the obsession of a pioneer, she cleared and planted with flowers. With flowers, only flowers. Phlox, larkspur, marguerites, irises; dahlias, too, eventually. Like before, when her father was alive, she entertained guests. She cooked like a goddess, the guests enthused by her art. As in the past, she sat at the table, observing the diners from the corner of her eye to make sure everything was fine; it was just that, now, there were no servants to pick up any dropped serviette. She'd to do it herself, and did so with a stiff grace. Edwin and his wife were not ever invited; but the cellist, who not even six years later would be murdered, was always present, as was Wern. Later, he stayed away; my mother didn't know why. He was probably going round the world. The other guests were no longer musicians, no longer artists. Normal people, just. Nonetheless, once (the German troops had just marched into the Rhineland) she managed to organize a fabulous shish-kebab night, a veritable food orgy, at which the guests took a seat on blankets in the grass, and turned their skewers in fires that were burning in long hollows. The wine was flowing, a full moon was behind the trees, and people were singing. It was just like before again, almost. — A letter arrived once from Edwin. It was written on handmade paper, in purple ink, and informed my mother that Edwin was pleased to inform her that she'd been made an honorary member of the Young Orchestra. Kind regards, E. (Later, the Orchestra had more honorary members. They were all composers, and close to Edwin. Their names were on a marble slab, hanging in the vestibule of the Historical Museum; and later in the Stadthalle. Bartók, Honegger, Stravinsky, Martin, Hinde-mith. And at the very top, my mother's name. She may not have shown it, but each time she went to a concert, she very much enjoyed glancing up at the Roman letters that high-lighted her name.) The honorary membership entitled her to free admission to the concerts for life. My mother sat on her old seat in the second row, behind Edwin.

HER idolization of Edwin did not kick in immediately; not at all. She wanted to be content, and she was. She had a house! She was somebody's wife! She became an outstanding house-wife, there wasn't a speck of dust in her home. She ironed with the precision of a watchmaker, had a place for her bedlinen, another for the kitchen towels, the stalks of the apples on the fruit and vegetable rack all pointed up. At the same time, she could accept the corner they worked in not ever getting tidied. It bothered her, but she knew, and reminded herself every day, that others had the right to be different. Toys, when toys then came along, weren't allowed to lie around, however, not ever, building blocks on the floor of the playroom would never have happened. A good meal was always put on the table, she'd the gift of being able to cook a mouth-watering meal, using only *cervelat* sausage, a few potatoes and a handful of chives. Herbs, spices, sauces: she was a champion when it came to these. She no longer had a car, but soon had a bicycle she used to do the shopping, with a wicker basket on the front handlebars. She would ride along, her dress blowing in the wind, a little shaky. She knew no fear and went down the steep road that her house was at the top of, much too fast. She rang her bell where others would brake. More than once, she ended up in wheat fields and nettles. Otherwise, as I said, she'd be in the garden, surrounded by blue smoke as a fire was always burning. There were always old leaves, or there was new wood, to be destroyed. She would poke around in the embers with a rake. Often, too, she'd just be standing there, leaning on the shaft and staring into the flames, and it may be that there, in the heat, in the smoke, in the swirling ash, her lips first began to move. Slowly at first, hesitantly, not immediately knowing what they wanted to say. At some point, though, the words arrived: Edwin. Edwin. Edwin. Edwin. Every fibre in my mother's body called 'Edwin'. Soon all the birds were singing 'Edwin', any water was gurgling his name. The wind whispered it, the sun burned it into her skin. 'Edwin', 'Edwin' from every plant, from every creature. 'Edwin!', distant dogs howled. 'Edwin!', drummed the rain. 'Edwin!', sang the engine of the Citroen in which, every morning, the Banga company delivered a pathetic litre of milk to this, the very last house in the town. The driver would say something to my mother, surely not Edwin; she knew, however, what she'd heard, and smiled. Edwin, only ever Edwin. She whispered the beloved syllables, too, of course, when she was peeling potatoes or lying, hoping to sleep, in her marital bed. Often, she would stand at a window, always the same one, and look into the distance, a sun-tanned Isolda, her hair all over the place, waiting for a white sail to emerge from the forest. For there, behind the forest that protected her from avalanches, lay the fortunate lake that got to reflect Edwin's image. — In a corner of the bedroom stood a table, a harmless little corner table, but *she* knew it was an altar. Or was it the opposite, was she the only person who didn't realize? On the table, anyway: two candles that never burned; the old, and also the newest programmes of the Young Orchestra, placed carefully, one on top of the other; the orchid, still fresh in April and early May, later withered; the small cards with the purple ink; and a framed photo of everyone involved in the legendary guest performance in Paris. My mother was the only one not in the picture; someone, after all, had had to take the photo. In the middle of the front row beamed Edwin, who had put one arm round the cellist, the other round the blond harpist. — At some point, my mother started taking walks that always led to this lake, to a pebble beach where a few boats lay, the small boats of the fishermen. Opposite, on the other side of the lake, flashed the roofs of Edwin's estate. — Later still, she took her walks at night too. In the moonlight, but also when there was no moon, she would walk through the forest, the four or five kilometres down to the lake, with a stone in her hands that she'd dug during the day from the garden, and that was so heavy that it was really tearing her arms out. That was how she went, and always to the lake. Reaching the shore, she didn't stop but waded far enough into the water for her legs to get completely wet, and her stomach more or less wet. Only then would she stand still, her knees knocking, her lips trembling, her eyes dry, saying Edwin, and staring across to the opposite shore. The stone would slip from her grasp, without her noticing. She would remain there like that. Finally, she'd do a right turn — perhaps because a night bird gave a call, or a distant car tooted its horn — hobble back to the shore and race home. Breathless, her legs still wet, and without the slightest sound, she would climb back into the bed she shared with her husband and lie, rigid, on her back, her eyes open. When the sun rose, she'd collapse into a short sleep and was dead beat if, much later, the noise of the day didn't rouse her. — When, in the evening, her guests arrived, she was beautiful. She received each and every one of them with perfect sincerity, and talked a lot, a lot, and loudly. Sometimes she raised her skirts and underskirts, without shame, up to her thighs, to show how she'd injured herself, falling off her bicycle. Scabs, dried-in blood, everywhere. She'd laugh so much, her girlfriends and other friends would laugh too.

OF course, she continued to yearn for I Leoni; now all the more. Just weeks after the wedding, already, she set out, alone, with her usual suitcase. This time, however, neither her uncles nor Boris found the time to fetch her from the station (was she a nobody in their eyes, maybe?), with the result that she'd to make her way on foot across the plain and up into the slopes of the vineyards. Five kilometres, more like eight. It was hot. Swarms of flies were buzzing round her. Clouds of dust when a car passed. The sun burning, no shade. (Was her way of life wrong?) Though the grasses and bushes were green this time, too; the flowers were blooming again; the lizards were once more darting along the stone walls; dragonflies were flying around like in the old days; and even the birds were chirping as they'd always done; my mother wasn't as thrilled as in the past when, finally, she climbed the steep, straight track to I Leoni. She was exhausted, sweating, and her feet were burning so much that she took her shoes off and walked the last hundred metres barefoot. (A punishment she deserved?) The estate, yellow, radiant, massive, rose before her. The church had been repainted, and the funny weeds on the gargoyles and in the gaps for the bells were gone. A strange noise from the terrace, the size of a church square, outside the house, and just high enough for my mother not to be able to see, as she approached, what was happening there. In pain, she climbed the front steps—broad steps, like outside a castle—and dropped her suitcase and shoes. She stood there, gasping. Looked round. Teeming with people, it was. Shouts, calls, everyone seemed to be roaring orders at everyone else and couldn't have cared less about any order just received. ('Coo hoo, I'm here!' Did no one see her?) Closest to her were three men, their trumpets gleaming golden, practising on a wooden platform, coming in again and again, a fanfare, jubilation, blasting out a sequence of notes, in any case, that didn't sound as proud as intended. Behind them, men and women, some of the servants, were putting up long wooden tables, one next to the other, then spreading white tablecloths over them and putting out plates, glasses, knives and forks. A girl was strewing flowers from a large basket. She was wearing a traditional costume decorated with ribbons and embroidery, yes, they were all dressed up, the maids and servants all looked like they would have done in former times. Jerkins, jackets, tuckers. They bristled with cleanliness. (My mother felt filthy.) Four men, panting, cursing, were positioning a wine cask the size of a house. The smaller of her two little uncles ran past, so close my mother could smell his breath. (Was she invisible?) He had a black shirt on, her smallest uncle, a red armband with very angular symbols, and was barking at two women who were decorating a triumphal arch made of wooden slats— my mother was directly beneath it—with wisteria umbels and roses. The women didn't respond to him, and her smallest uncle turned to the wine cask instead. Boris was now standing there; he, too, barely recognizable. He wasn't just wearing a black shirt, he was wearing an actual uniform, it black too, and he'd a riding crop in his right hand, a small whip that, when he shouted an order, he cracked in the air. The maids and servants were more likely to listen to him, oh yes, he exuded great strength, and what he wanted was clear. — Her smallest uncle sensed that too and again changed direction, heading for the kitchen this time. — My mother waved to Boris as he looked in her direction, but when their eyes met, he looked away and straightened up a chair. (She was invisible.) He then just stood there, his hands on his hips, and his neck craning so much, his pursed lips kissed the sky. Oh, Boris! — To one side, along the balustrade of the terrace, her big uncle was pacing up and down. He was in black too, but civilian clothing, a swish suit. And a tie! He was moving his lips, every now and then he punched his fist in the air, and he was squinting at a piece of paper he held in his hand. No doubt about it, he was practising. He didn't see my mother either, though his vacant gaze seemed to land on her again and again. — Uncle No. 3 did not reappear. More in blue than in black, he was probably in the kitchen, minding the bottle of grappa. Her aunt swept past my mother, her eyes focused on an arrangement of ears of corn and terracotta grapes, painted a garish blue, that was lying on the terrace balustrade. '*Reto, Renzo, rapido!*' those *r*'s now sounding even more like hissing vipers. My mother ran a few steps behind her aunt, then stopped. (As if she didn't exist.) — The shouts, calls, only calmed down, faded, once the tablecloths had all vanished beneath the flowers and the glasses were all sparkling equally in the sunlight. Once the chairs were lined up like Guards. Once none of the wood in the arch remained visible. Once the trumpeters were standing at ease on their platform, the trumpets on their shoulders like rifles. Once her big uncle, with a sigh, put his piece of paper in his jacket pocket. Once her smallest uncle came back from the kitchen, with an absent smile and wiping his mouth. Once her aunt took off her apron, revealing a russet, silk evening dress. Once the servants gathered in groups, across the terrace, as if posing for a painting. Once Boris straightened the belt and straps of his uniform, and brushed a fleck of invisible dust from his sleeve. And once, above all, an excited voice shouted 'They're coming! They're coming!' The voice was that of Uncle No. 3 who, sober as a judge, was at a first-floor window and pointing into a distance concealed from those on the terrace. 'There they are! About to enter the columns!' Round-mouthed, Boris inhaled all the air he could muster, his chest swelled, he rocked back and forth on his feet—he was wearing boots!—cast a last glance round the house, tables and servants and spotted my mother who was still, if now a few steps away from her suitcase and shoes, beneath the arch. He raced over to her.

'Clara?! What are you doing here?'

'I . . .'

'What do you look like? He mustn't see you like this!'

'Who?'

He grabbed her arm—'Come on! Come with me!'—dragged her with him, so quickly, she was falling into the back of him. Only in the darkness of the gate to the house did Boris stop, and my mother too. 'It's a great day!' he shouted. 'He's visiting I Leoni. He'll be here any minute!' His eyes shone. 'Go to your room. And don't come out until it's all over!'

And at that, Boris rushed diagonally across the terrace, back to the staircase, to the triumphal arch, where he took up position alongside her big uncle. My mother went into the house. (Why shouldn't the important visitor see her?) She felt her way through the dark hall and climbed the — dimly lit — stairs. Went along corridors, turning off this way, that way. The silence of the former monastery making her footsteps echo all the more. The cool air. Finally, her cell. She opened the door and smelled the familiar dust. Bed, table, wash bowl, cupboard. The picture with the shepherd boy. She sighed (was she now a disgrace?) and opened the window. The light and the heat hit her immediately, like a blow. In the distance, an unfamiliar rumbling. She leaned out. Far below: the terrace, the tables, the servants in groups. Boris and her big uncle, they too motionless now, like *tableaux vivants*. On the path my mother had just walked, a long snake of dust was crawling towards I Leoni. Its head, preceding the dust, was a car full of pennants and spare tyres, a monstrous carriage made of armour plates. Behind the driver, who was wearing a cap and racing goggles, stood a man in a white uniform, swaying to and fro. He raised his hand, pointed at the vines or the gods. In the cloud of dust behind him, parts of other vehicles were visible, phantom-like, for seconds at a time: a wheel here, part of a bonnet, a dust-coloured pennant. Men's iron faces, some coughing. The approaching armada rumbled more audibly, soon became loud, was now roaring, and when the car with the white hero reached the gravel below the terrace staircase, the trumpeters couldn't get their trumpets to their lips quickly enough, to play. Boris stormed down the steps. The servants shrieked with delight, threw their hats in the air, and a chorus of boys and girls started to sing. Happy faces, the eyes beaming. The driver of the first car stopped, got out, opened the car door, saluted, and the white god stepped down onto this earth. He was small and fat, his neck broader than his skull. He raised his chin when he saw Boris racing towards him, he too with a chin that looked like a shovel. (Since when did Boris have such massive jawbones?) Boris, in any case, raised one arm sharply, barked something, and the guest raised one arm too. He puckered his lips, like a fish, or as if he, too, wanted to kiss the sky—like Boris had done— then they shook hands. For a long time, and firmly. (Why was Boris ashamed of her?) In the meantime—they were standing wherever there was space—men in black uniforms had got out of the other cars. Many men. Just men. All in black.— Her big uncle had remained at the top of the steps, beneath the arch, and greeted the guest by bowing several times. The guest raised his arm again, this time, however, as if he were tired of all these salutes, such constant reverence. He wanted to be himself now. Her big uncle held his speech nonetheless, with his piece of paper in his hand, but without consulting it. My mother couldn't hear what he was saying, but she could see him, the white guest too, how he was standing there, moving his lips, as if his palate were testing the quality of these words in his honour. Boris was standing with his gob wide open. When her uncle was finished, the guest nodded, took a step, and stumbled over my mother's suitcase. He didn't fall, at least; but wobbled a bit until he regained his balance. And stood there, his eyes bulging—everyone else was rooted to the spot—and suddenly started laughing. Was roaring with laughter from within that broad chest of his that his right hand was thumping. The men in black applauded. Their master, how self-sure he was! How relaxed was his response to life's wrongs. — Boris hissed at her little uncle, who took the suitcase and ran into the house with it while Boris lifted the shoes and hurled them into the fig trees. (So that was how he was treating her now?) — Meanwhile, they were all sitting at the long tables; the white guest between her big uncle and her aunt, who was the only woman. Boris, her other neighbour, bent across her to shout a joke in the guest's direction, and all credit to him, the latter nodded, beaming. Steam was rising from huge plates on the tables, mountains of meat, gigantic pieces. Polenta in large bowls. Salads. They drank to each other's health, emptied their glasses with manly gulps. Soon, great merriment prevailed, the men showing they could celebrate, were carefree and jolly. They were all capable of earthy humour, as my mother realized even from high above them. Of being tough and strict also, of course, —if that was necessary, of course. When the white guest removed the jacket of his uniform and put it over his chair, one or other of the men undid his top button too. Roars of laughter, again and again. Red faces. — My mother was hungry and thirsty and looked to see if there was any water in the pitcher for washing, or in the other cells, somewhere. (They begrudged her even water.) She thus missed the guests getting up to leave. For when she returned to the window and looked down, they were all rushing to their automobiles. It was as if events had overtaken them, a distant battle cry, maybe. The sound of doors closing, the engines. While the last of their fellow soldiers were still emptying their glasses at the tables, the white guest's car was already driving off. Was he Il Duce? (My God, that was Il Duce, she was seeing Il Duce with her own eyes.) He'd sunk deep into his cushion — his head could barely be seen now — and was staring ahead. He'd already forgotten I Leoni. Nevertheless, Boris was running, waving, alongside the car and only stopped down in the vines. He disappeared in the dust of the escorts' cars. He coughed. Coughed and coughed as the roaring of Il Duce's army faded. Finally, he emerged from the fog of dust again, as brown as the track itself, he wheezed and choked another two or three times, then rubbed his eyes. The others, too — her uncle, aunt and servants — came out from under the spell and entered the house. The sounds from earlier returned. Cocks crowing, dogs barking and, in the distance, a death knell.

THE next day Boris kept the promise he'd made to my mother on her first visit: they climbed the Cima Bianca. In the middle of the night still, they set out for the mountains in the

Skoda, and—at sunrise—were already on an alp, high above the valleys. They parked the car outside an empty stable. Golden morning light. My mother felt her heart beat as she looked up to the chain of mountain peaks above her, the highest of which, that is, Cima Bianca, had a white cap. Phew. The south face, rising into the sky right in front of them, was still regarded as unconquerable, though Boris had climbed it solo. Today, though, they wanted to take the normal route. Boris, nonetheless, had his pickaxe and rope with him, and my mother sighed so loudly he put an arm round her shoulders and laughed. 'Everything will be all right, girl!' They took themselves off, silent, and with those slow steps that on harmless terrain look almost ridiculous, and yet help to keep your strength for when you get to the top. Wet grass, dewdrops catching the morning sun, the gurgle of streams. A marmot whistled. Soon, the first snow patches. Two hours later, they were at the foot of the ridge, solid rock now. Debris, sparse flowers here and there, the last mountain finches they'd see, a slight wind. Sun, more sun, the world was shining. My mother was gasping for breath whereas Boris, ahead of her, was dancing to the top. Far below, the vapours of the plain in the morning heat; but up here it was chilly. 'Oh!' Boris shouted. 'What a day!' My mother said nothing, she was too out of breath. But she too was more and more reconciled. Boris was so strong! So sure! So certain!—At the large field of snow, they roped themselves up. Boris now went far ahead, belayed with the pick, and had my mother follow. She kept her eyes on his footprints, didn't look down once. The snow crunched beneath their feet. Later, there were parts where you had to clamber, the first stage, then *il camino*, the ridge, easy to climb. My mother was glad nonetheless, though, that Boris was above her, pulling her up on the rope. How certain he was! The world, below, was far away. White clouds on the horizon. Boris remained calm even when my mother slipped once; the shock for a moment as her foot was hanging over the precipice. He held her on the rope, and beamed at her. Soon, they were standing below the last rock — perpendicular, it rose straight into the air, but then proved not so hard to climb — and soon after that, they reached the summit. The snow as hard as ice. A cast iron cross, two rusty tins beneath it. A panorama — as far as Africa and Greenland, nearly. Summits, ridges, peaks, glaciers with a blue sheen. Only straight in front of them did an even higher mountain rise into the sky, a massive block that my mother didn't recognize as the Matterhorn because, from this side, it didn't look like it. Boris had sat down on a stone and unpacked the picnic. Bread, the local air-dried meat and dried apricots. Tea. 'We are living in great times,' he said, chewing his bread. 'I am proud to be allowed to be part of this new force.' He pointed with his chin — he'd that shovel again now! — towards the south. 'Abyssinia is ours! The land of our forefathers! Isn't it splendid? That it's now our turn? We young ones? I'll take I Leoni to the top. I'll force Ruffino to his knees, and Antinori! I will!' He was aglow, and my mother nodded violently. Boris could be so passionate. 'How magnificent it is up here!' she exclaimed. 'Away from all the people!' In the fire of their enthusiasm, neither had noticed that the white clouds—just recently, still distant and small,—had become huge mountains of cloud, now towering over them. A wind sprang up. They put their rucksacks on, and set about the descent. This time, my mother went first, and Boris belayed behind her. They were now making slower progress, of course. My mother often groped for the correct hold and hesitated even if Boris was giving the clearest of instructions. Now, he sounded impatient at times. By the time the ridge was behind them, the wind had become a storm, and the clouds above them black and menacing. Neither of them said a word, but they went quickly, more quickly perhaps than careful belaying allowed. They did the *camino* and the first stage at the double, as it were. Once, indeed, Boris stepped onto a ledge so rashly, it thundered down into the abyss, a torrent of stones in its wake. As they reached the first stage and were able to see the large field of snow again, the thunderstorm started. Lightning flashed from the clouds, the thunderclaps crashing simultaneously. It started to rain. My mother felt the rope holding her back and turned round. A few steps behind, Boris was cowering in the scree. He'd thrown his pick away, and his arms were hugging his head. My mother went back to him. Boris was trembling, shaking, and when my mother touched his arm, he screamed. He was sobbing now, crying, his body jerking wildly as if the whirlwind were raging within him. 'Boris,' my mother said. 'Boris.' The lightning was striking above them, below them, to their right, to their left—making my mother duck too. The rain was like an ice-cold whip. Boris had his head between his knees and was whimpering to himself. He was stinking really badly now. Soaked to the skin long since, they stayed in that position. Boris' teeth were chattering. My mother felt uneasy too. Thunderbolts, two flashes, five flashes, simultaneously, the thunder breaking all at once, and so loudly, you thought it was inside your head. This went on for an eternity. Finally, the thunder was more distant, the lightning less frequent, the rain poured down with less finality. My mother stood up. Boris was now lying in a cleft in the rock. Was he dead? She shook him. 'Everything will be all right,' she said. Boris didn't move, but groaned. 'Take your underpants off,' my mother said. 'I won't look.' As she watched the lightning, far off already, and striking in the plain now, she heard Boris—indeed—get up. He was fiddling around, and suddenly started blubbering. Then, though, a cloth bundle did fly past and down into the depths. It smacked onto a rock. 'Give me your hand,' my mother said. She helped Boris across the large field of snow, down the debris, to the foot of the ridge. On the meadows, Boris was able to walk unaided again, but was still crying so much, he was tripping over stones, and stepping into puddles. Somehow they reached the alp. My mother hustled Boris into the passenger seat in the Skoda, and got behind the wheel. As she drove down the alp road, the sun was shining again. Down in the plain, they drove along between poplars that looked like silhouettes, with the setting sun behind them. 'My father,' Boris said, suddenly quite loudly, 'isn't afraid of thunderstorms.' Then he was silent again. When they arrived at I Leoni, it was dark. The headlights lit up the house, and then Boris, as he stumbled to the door. My mother drove the Skoda into the garage, climbed up to her cell, took her wet things off and ate the rest of the picnic.

THEN her child came into the world, me, and this time she wanted to be allowed to be pleased. She wanted to be pleased, pleased whenever she looked at her child. Bathed it, breast-fed it. Rocked it, sang to it, fondled it, hugged it. Took it for a walk. Showed it the beautiful world, the sun, the light. — But she couldn't, simply didn't manage to. No light, no sun. There was no milk from her breast, her songs stopped before the end, and when she kissed her child, she threatened to smother it. She didn't laugh, no. On the contrary. All day, every day, she sobbed without tears, screamed without making a sound. By night, sleepless and hitting out, she fought off her dreams, but when morning came, she clutched at precisely these night-mares — as if they could help her — in order not to have to enter the new day. She would press her eyes shut though she'd already been awake for a long time. Even if the child was screaming. When she then did get up after all, finally, it was as if she were in a daze. As white as chalk, and with tangled hair, she crept along the walls, still in her dressing gown in the evening. She didn't hear anyone calling, didn't answer. Did she see where she was going? Her manner now, in any case, was to tremble as she drank a glass of water, to shake when cutting bread. To jump out of her chair with fright when the telephone rang. She would forget to cook or, at an inopportune moment, serve a lavish dish. She would support herself on the hotplate and not notice that her hand was braising. Conversely, she would air the rooms for hours when it was freezing cold outside. She couldn't bring herself to utter the word *sterben*, meaning 'to die'—incredibly, always said *stürbseln*—while, in her head, running through her list of ways to die, again and again. By drinking rat poison from the shed. By slashing her wrists with the kitchen knife. By swallowing pills, all at once, by drinking whisky, every drop she had, then going out into the snow and lying down beneath the walnut tree. By scalding herself in the bath. By going into the lake and not stopping this time, not letting go of the stone.—The child she wanted to take with her, that went without saying. 'Taking the child with her' was what she called it.—She stood at the window and pressed her forehead against the glass. The window steaming up where her mouth was. Outside, the lilacs were blooming, the countryside was shimmering in the summer, the stubble-fields were resplendent or the snow was gleaming up as far as the forest: she would see no difference. She wrung her hands and whispered to herself. Yes, that was the worst part, the way she whispered. A ghost, she would whisper right through the house. Would hiss from the cellar, having only just been on the roof. Her rustling would arrive ahead of her, all this whispering, first the whisper would be there, and then her. Her lips would move in never-ending prayer. Anyone meeting her in the corridor would step into the middle—she, of course, was creeping along the walls—

and try to understand what she was saying; wouldn't, however, understand. Accusations, revenge, justifications? — She thought flames were leaping from her skin; or that vermin were devouring her from within. — Now, when she stood in the lake — she always did so at night, carrying the child instead of the stone — her eyes latched onto the windows of Edwin's house, gleaming in the distance. She saw only these lights, how they shone, how they glistened. Stars, they were, and so enticing. — Her child, that — like the stone before — she had let go, would clutch at her dress. Not that it bothered her, she didn't notice. — She would stare greedily, so enraptured that the distant palace would seem to come closer and closer, get bigger and bigger, more and more real. Yes, soon she was standing at the railings round the garden, she, Clara, long-lost Clara, peering up the slanting torch-lit lawn to the castle windows. Shadows behind the glass. Music, muffled laughter. Were there dogs? Even if there were, she didn't care. They were just what she needed, these mastiffs, let them come and tear her to pieces. As she lay there in her white dress, her throat bitten, the grass red with her blood! — She darted across the lawn, past the burning torches, pulled herself up on the trellis, and looked into the castle. Oh, what splendour. A room full of gold, lit by a thousand candles in the chandeliers. A long table with guests. Gentlemen in dinner jackets, ladies in evening dresses, with marvellous chests, above which diamonds sparkled. That one there was the lady of the house. She was beautiful. Oh yes, she was wonderful. She was sitting in a wedding dress at the centre of the table, a single jewel shining, red, above her décolleté neckline. She was smiling and chatting, and yet her eyes were giving directions to all the servants. My mother could see exactly what was happening. The raising of an eyebrow, a quick glance, and they dashed over to this corner, that corner, topping up wine, or bringing a new fork. She did it wonderfully. Perfectly! Edwin was sitting beside her. Was he wearing white gloves? A ruched white dress shirt, in any case, for sure. A black sheen to his hair, and a perfect parting. His nose, more than ever, that of a bird of prey. He leaned over his wife and said something amorous. How his eyes sparkled! How hers shone! The way they sat together, looking deeply into each other's eyes as if the other guests weren't there. Edwin's eyes were steel blue, his wife's twinkled darkly. — But what was that? My mother — her heart racing with excitement — now saw that it was she herself who was sitting beside Edwin. She, yes, she! Edwin turned to her, yes, to *her*! — Suddenly, she woke up, perhaps because her child's head had now also entered the water, and it was hitting out. She lifted me up and trudged back to the shore. Wet all over, her legs, her stomach. Leaving a trail of water behind, she ran back home and threw me and herself into bed. — She now often bit her lips until they bled, had trickles of dried-in blood on her chin. Her child fled from her, that is: I did, and yet held his little arms out to her. — Around this time, the Young Orchestra announced the premiere of a new piece by Béla Bartók. Bartók had written it for Edwin, as a commission. (In his holiday chalet near Adelboden, to be precise. Bartók, thrilled by the experience, had spent four weeks in a room smelling of old wood, and with no access to newspapers. He'd missed a thing or two, the beginning of the Second World War included. Edwin drove up to him in his Rolls and reported the unimaginable. Bartók nodded, shook his head, gulped; on the other hand, though, he'd not yet orchestrated the end of his piece, and had to get straight back down to work.) My mother ran a bath and undressed and got into the hot water and soaped herself and rinsed herself again and washed her hair and dried it for an hour or more with the hair-dryer and put it up into something like a castle. She powdered herself and applied make-up from head to toe and put on her black silk dress. A necklace from when her father was still alive. Her coat with the fur collar and a hat with a veil. This was how she sat in her usual seat in the second row — the concerts were still being held in the Historical Museum. Her head at an angle. Smiling. Edwin was standing right in front of her on a kind of crate, and she was staring at the tails of his tailcoat bobbing up and down. She didn't hear a single note. She felt dizzy. When Edwin lowered the baton and let the final notes fade, it was as if he had cast a spell on the entire audience. A deep silence, never-ending almost. Incredible applause then erupted. Bartók's piece — Divertimento for String Orchestra — was a master-piece, and the audience recognized the gift they had been offered. They clapped and clapped, didn't want to stop. This time the back of the room, too, was enchanted; those who had once booed and whistled were now standing, cheering and laughing to each other. My mother, too, was clapping. 'Bravo,

bravo, yes,' my mother got up and shouted 'Bravo!' Bartók, again shook everyone's hands, and Edwin nodded in his usual fashion to the audience, as if any expression of gratitude would have a price attached. The musicians were tapping their bows on their instruments. The cellist was sitting in the front row. (She was glowing with happiness. This was her last concert with the Young Orchestra. She was heading off to Berlin, to the man she loved.) — After the concert — it was snowing heavily — my mother was standing outside the Historical Museum, waiting for a taxi, when the side door opened and Bartók stepped out. He was wearing a heavy coat and blinking up at the snowflakes, and then came straight up towards my mother. 'Béla!' she called, taking a step towards him. Bartók stared at her, said, 'Thank you, thank you', and walked past her. My mother called, 'It's me, Clara!' — and the door opened again. Edwin. 'Through here, Béla!' he shouted, waving. His voice was like a general's, and he looked at my mother, unmoved. Bartók did a right turn and, beaming with pleasure, ran towards him. Edwin put an arm round his shoulders. And thus they walked off, big Edwin and little Béla, through the rain that was pouring from the heavens, and they disappeared, at the far end of the street, into the restaurant. Zum Goldenen Löwen. That night, my mother sat on the couch, biting into a cushion, and shouting 'I can't take it any more!' She hit her head off the wall. She couldn't take it any more. A doctor was called, and she was taken away, a whimpering bundle, with her coat with the fur collar round her shoulders. Her child, I, rolled along behind the patient being moved, climbed down the precipice of each step in the stairs, and, finally, also made it out. Snow, in the light of the hall. In it, fat tracks, vanishing in the dark. The garden gate, visible still, was open.

IT remained open, no one closed it. There was no wind to move it. Sparrows fell, dead, from the sky. The sun was black, the moon blind. There was no one about on earth. The water in the streams had frozen. Dead trout stared out of the ice. Clouds were hanging in the trees. The grass was grey. Dust— volcanic ash maybe—on every path. In the gardens, mice were lying on their backs, cats, frozen over them, in mid flow. Frost patterns on the windows. Not a sound anywhere, no crows cawing, nothing. The world was silent. The house, a grave.—Then my mother came back. Electric shocks had been used to cure her. (Once, later, much later, she said—just once she said it!—that electrotherapy was the worst thing that ever happened to her. She'd been taken into a chamber. Green walls, no windows. Light from the ceiling, no furniture, apart from a narrow couch. Dark imitation leather, straps, metal clips. Equipment, cables. She was strapped—three men in white coats were there, she resisted, if half-heartedly—to the bed. Straps round her legs, straps round her wrists. She lay there, silent, rigid, felt something tighten round her skull. A kind of helmet. A piece of rubber was forced into her mouth. She now wanted to scream, did whine, made noises. The doctors, though, didn't bother with her, just spoke across her. 'Shall I start with ninety?'—'I'd say so, yes. We can always go higher.'—The electric shock was like an explosion. A flash in her head, a whip lashing through every muscle. She writhed, bit into the rubber, forced her eyes shut, tore them open again. Howled inwardly, like a wolf; she *was* a wolf. A storm within her until she lay there motionless; remaining so, once the fetters were undone. The piece of rubber was taken out, her mouth stayed open. 'Okay. That's us finished.' She was moved back to her room where she lay on her back, staring at the ceiling. Every morning she was brought to the treatment room, often enough for her—now an empty shell—to start lying down of her own accord, putting her hands, without hesitation, in the leather fetters. For her to feel as much before the electric shock as she did afterwards; as little. The rest of the time, she lay in her white room—light, more light, the curtains moving in the breeze; it was spring again—until one of the doctors came and told her she was healthy and could go home again. 'Isn't it wonderful you're now so well again?' And so my mother got up, packed her nightdress and toothbrush in her little case, took her coat with the fur collar from the hanger, and went home where her child, me, was still, or again, in the doorway and wet himself when she appeared at the open gate.)—Now, the sun was shining again, the trees were in blossom, the grass a bright green. Invisible, in the distance—invisible for the moment— was the war. (Hitler had ravaged Poland.) My mother put her case in the bedroom, hung her coat in the wardrobe, put on her oldest dress and her mountain boots, and went into the garden. She felled the lilac tree and the whitethorn, and ripped out all the narcissi, tulips, daffodils, irises and cowslips. With a spade, she turned over the flower garden she'd just cleared—a bare field now, from one horizon to the other—without any help. There were no men any more. She broke the clods of earth up with a hoe, throwing all the stones—a great many, countless, the field was very rocky—on a pile that soon became a mountain. She raked the broken-up clay, again and again, and then once more. Until it was grainy; flour-like almost. (At Dunkirk, Hitler hounded the British into the sea.) My mother dug holes with a dibble, made furrows with the back of her hand. She scattered seeds from small packets, and pressed seedlings into the earth. Watered them, individually, with rainwater that wasn't too cold, taking it from a rusty drum, surrounded by a little marsh, beside the tool shed. Walking at a slant, with one arm in the air, she dragged watering cans from which the water splashed. She rammed wooden poles into the ground, long ones for the climbing beans, and short ones for the peas. Beneath the chestnut tree and the beech tree she spread cloths out and, standing on a ladder, beat the cockchafers down. Thousands of brown beetles (Hitler marched into Paris, his arm extended, in the air) that she filled into buckets and, for five rappen per litre, brought to the collection point by bike, the buckets either side of the handlebars; she was thrown from her bike several times, of course, into the nettles where the beetles disappeared. — The dog was always around somewhere too, she now had a dog. — She tied the tomatoes up with yellow bast and broke off the shoots she didn't want. She put wood wool beneath the still green strawberries. She sprayed poison. (Hitler bombed Coventry to bits.) She ran with the wheelbarrow, full of peat or old leaves, along the paths between the vegetable patches, paths the width of her feet. Yes, she ran, she didn't ever walk. She forced the garden hose into a mouse hole, turned the water on, and used her shovel to kill the mice that fled from the other holes. (Hitler had now reached Narvik too, the North Pole, or almost.) With one of her buckets and a shovel in hand, she followed the farmers' horses, collecting the droppings. She picked camomile from alongside the paths and dried it on cloths. On all her windowsills lay half-green, half-red tomatoes. The aroma of them! The granite slabs in the path to the garden gate were burning hot! Lizards would vanish between the stones! Every now and then, my mother would straighten up—she was always bent over a barrel of rose-hip syrup or a weed—and, turning her upper lip up, would blow down her blouse. Even she was finding it hot! Mosquitoes, the drone of mosquitoes was everywhere. Swarms of flies round her head. Crouching between the green plants, she hunted Colorado beetles. She would dig out mole-hills and crush cockchafer grubs with her foot. Mole crickets, if ever a mole cricket flew over the vegetable patches, you'd hear her scream! (Now Mussolini went mad too, marched into Greece.) On the compost heap, more of a mountain, huge cucumbers were growing. Courgettes and zucchetti, resembling primeval creatures, were bulging over each other. (Hitler met Pétain, who was wearing a feathered hat.) When it got colder, when rain poured down, my mother, wrapped in a black cape, would crouch among the potatoes and dig them out. She filled crate after crate and, with a rolling gait, carried them down to the cellar. She would string onions together and hang them up in the shed. Even with the door closed, you could smell the strings of onions, the scent went as far as the water drum that smelled of moss. At harvest-time there was no festival, my mother didn't do festivals. But apples, pears, quince and nuts were piled up everywhere. My mother would stand in the kitchen, making jam. Steam. There was no sugar, but she got some from somewhere. It was just for the preserves, though, not for sweet things. Cellophane, red rubber rings. For the bottled pears, apricots and plums, she had green jars from Bülach. That they were from Bülach was somehow important. — She cleaned, ran, cooked, scrubbed. Rose with the sun — she who, once, had been too fond of her bed — and lay down at midnight. — Then snow fell. Now — if she wasn't clearing the paths or stamping around in the sauerkraut barrel — she would sit in the one room she was prepared to heat, and that she called 'the warmth'. She would sew trousers, darn socks, knit pullovers and clean the old silver, the silver from before, until it glistened and sparkled and shone. She'd then lock it away again; she never used it to eat. — She no longer went to the lake. From time to time, she would just stop at the little table, the altar; but not really praying. At most, she would flick through a programme, then put it back. Sometimes she'd stand at the window and look across at the forest. But *rarely*, you'd have to say it was rarely. — This was how she lived. Hitler attacked Russia and my mother planted onions. Hitler laid siege to Moscow. My mother pulled out turnips. Rommel's tanks chased Montgomery's across the Sahara. My mother stood in the smoke from a fire that put an end to old branches. Hitler reached the Don. My mother in among the corn. Stalingrad! My mother sewed black curtains, put them up in all the windows and, trudging through snow, checked from outside to ensure no light whatsoever was getting through. The Americans took Sicily. My mother stood, wringing her hands, at the sight of tomatoes rotting before they ripened. The Americans, the British, the Canadians and the French landed in Normandy. My mother removed a silvery film from the beans. De Gaulle, bigger than everyone else, marched into Paris, leading his troops, while my mother was feeding the rabbits. When the Allies reached the Rhine, my mother was filling the fruit and vegetable racks in the cellar with russet apples. And when Hitler, crazier than ever, gave the command for the Ardennes Offensive, my mother was chopping a young fir down in the forest — at dusk, so as the forester didn't catch her — because it was Christmas and my mother had never ever spent Christmas without a tree with candles. The Russians fought their way through to Berlin, and my mother was getting new vegetable patches ready. On 8 May 1945, around midday, all the bells were ringing. In the distance, beyond the horizon — my mother didn't live near a church. It was as if the earth itself were ringing. My mother dropped the hoe she'd been using to break up clay onto the ground, and sat down on the garden bench that, for five years, had served only as a place for her gardening clothes or the hedge-clippers. She breathed in, breathed out. The cherry trees were beginning to blossom, and the swallows were circling their nests. You could hear the goldfinches. The laburnum was flowing from its branches, the wisteria was in bloom. From far off, over the fields and up the road, black dots were approaching. Were getting bigger and, finally, big. The men. The men were returning, in their uniforms, with their knapsacks and carbines over their shoulders. They were laughing and waving, each and every one of them recognizable now. My mother raised her hand, waved too. 'Dog,' she said to the dog, 'From today, the two of us will have to pull through peacetime, we will.' She stood up, stepped over the child that was on the ground, using stones to build a castle, an impregnable fort, and went into the house.

THE war was over. Everyone who was still alive raised their heads and looked around, my mother too. What had become of the others? Far from the town, at its outermost edge, my mother didn't get to hear much. And so the first piece of news that was important didn't reach her until a burning day, at the height of summer. It came from Wern, from that very person. My mother met him at the gents' underpants bargain basket in EPA, a department store in the town centre. She blushed, — would have fled perhaps, had she been able to do so, unseen — as she'd been caught in a shop that a Lermitier lady or a Bodmer lady or Edwin's wife would never have entered. Not ever. Wern, who was holding flag-sized white underpants out from his stomach to gauge the size of them, was not in the least embarrassed, on the contrary. He was pleased to see her, hugged my red-faced mother and kissed her on both cheeks. 'Clara! How nice!' He was accompanied by an exotic-looking lady, a minute beauty with almond eyes and a radiant smile. She was from Bali, and his wife. It turned out both had arrived in town just two days before, after an adventurous trip on the backs of donkeys and on ships that had stopped in every, literally every, port, and so they'd been travelling for more than two months. They had set out on the day peace was declared. 'Why from Bali?' my mother said. Wern laughed, throwing the underpants back in the basket. 'Good luck, or bad luck, judge for yourself.' He'd been travelling through the South Seas when the war spread to Asia. No way of getting home. He made the best of the situation by wooing a young island beauty who, when he won her over, turned out to be the daughter of a local king. Wern told the latter he was a king back in Europe, and a conjurer who, by snapping his fingers, could make the greenfly ruining the king's plantations vanish. He snapped his fingers, sprayed his product, snapped his fingers again, and the king saw, with amazement, how his plants began to flourish. His daughter did too, the princess, and so he gave Wern her hand. Wern now lived in a luxury palm hut, slept in a hammock with golden threads, drank pineapple juice and sugarcane schnapps from elaborately carved bowls and smoked cigars he rolled himself, using local tobaccos—the only hint of bitterness in this chalice of complete and utter bliss. He loved his wife with a sexual appetite that was European, she responded to his passion with Balinese devotion. With music paper packed in his luggage, and huge big ears, he rode through jungles and over mountains to reach island villages in the back of beyond, transcribing everything he heard that sounded even remotely like music. The din of drums, tooting down pipes, blowing on reeds. Choral wailing. (And indeed, two years later, in September 1947, Gallimard in Paris published, in French, his *Abrégé de la Musique de l'Ile de Bali*, a fat volume of over two thousand pages, packed with music samples and analyses of the principles, that instantly became *the* book on the subject.) He collected anything and everything: masks, shields, door posts, canoes, an entire house for men. When, three years later, his collection reached the town in several trucks, it was an instant sensation and, in the Ethnological Museum, filled three rooms, from which considerable quantities of Roman tiles, medieval hearths and eighteenth-century pots were banished to the cellars. — Wern and his wife, at least temporarily, were now living in Edwin's old apartment which, following his wedding, he'd kept as a *pied à terre*. To relax in, between rehearsals, as a quiet place to work, and — Wern beamed at my mother — for the occasional adventure. 'Edwin and women, you know what he's like. He's still not one to miss a chance.' He roared with laughter, and my mother, too, managed a smile. There he was, then. Wern. Rounder than ever, beaming with happiness, and now he was even going so far as to *light* his cigar. His wife, he said, was thrilled to bits by his kingdom. By this—with an imperial gesture, he pointed at all the goods and customers—by all this. She thought, apparently, he ruled over all the sales assistants. As well as over the waiters in restaurants, the postman, the trams. He waved to his wife who was trying on a straw hat in front of a mirror. Forty per cent off, down to eight francs fifty. She looked delightful—in duplicate, thanks to the mirror. She had one of the magic notes supplied by Wern, and gave it to the underling at the till. In exchange, she was given a handful of shiny coins, and was allowed to keep the hat. She waved. Was jumping for joy, and laughing. Wern really was a powerful ruler. My mother accompanied them both out to the street and watched as, with their arms tightly round each other, they walked off, a royal couple in a cloud of smoke, for whom the underlings, respectfully, made way.—The local composer had died at some point in one of the cold winters of the war. Dying of hunger and thirst, he'd frozen to death. No one had noticed he'd died—it was the landlord, wanting his rent, who found him—no one came to the funeral. It poured with rain. Two employees from the cemeteries department carried him, at the double, to his grave, and it was a complete miracle that one of them, a student of music doing this as a part-time job, on the way back to the building where the service had been, was humming—he didn't know why, himself—the melody of the much-requested last of the Cinq Variations sur le thème Le ruisseau qui cours après toy-mesme de François Richard. Edwin, at any rate, had sent a wreath that now lay lonely and wet on the mound. On one ribbon, it said 'In Gratitude', on the other, 'The Young Orchestra'. On this one, attached with a paper clip, was a visiting card. Sweeping handwriting, purple ink. 'All the best, E.' The ink was running, tears, in long streaks, down onto the grave. — The leader of the Young Orchestra, the old hand, was no longer alive either. On the day on which general mobilization had been introduced — he'd been much too old for it — he'd suffered a stroke and then sat for three years in an armchair at his daughter's house, with his bow in his shaky right hand, and the violin itself on his knees. On a dull November evening, the latter fell to the floor and he stamped on it. Intentionally, or not. The next morning, he, too, was dead. — The cellist had been murdered in Buchenwald. She was three months pregnant when the Gestapo arrested her, and took her away, during a concert. When required to turn frozen earth over with a spade in the sleet, she screamed at the overseer — it screamed out of her — that she and her child would die, doing this. The overseer took the spade and battered them to death. Her and her child. — Sami Hirsch (who wrote to my mother, in English) had dragged his parents over into Switzerland, at the very last minute, and using force almost. To Basel, where they were given shelter by friends. The paintings and furniture he'd left behind in Frankfurt had been the price paid to the Nazis to let him and his parents go. The latter died almost right away, and simultaneously, nearly. He buried them, then somehow made his way — he was penniless and didn't have any valid documents — to Marseilles, and ended up, via Lisbon, in New York. There he qualified all over again, in English, and became a legal adviser at Sotheby's. 'I never will speak German again,' he wrote, in the letter. 'Sometimes, Clara, I dream of our swimming in the lake, in happier days. Sincerely yours, Sami.' — Ditta and Béla Bartók had also escaped to America. They, too, to New York. From day one, Bartók was thoroughly miserable and ill. He lay in hospital, gave a concert, landed in hospital again. When he found himself back in the Doctor's Hospital, a man he didn't know suddenly appeared at his bedside. He introduced himself as Serge Koussevitzky, the music director of the Boston Symphony Orchestra, no less — Bartók had heard of him, of course — and said his wife had died, yes, and he'd loved her like no one else on earth, and wanted Bartók to compose something in her memory. A requiem. Here was the cheque. Bartók, tired and weak, shook his head, and Koussevitzky left, disappointed. Then, though, Bartók sat for a whole summer in a room in a log cabin at Saranac Lake and composed the Concerto for Orchestra. Unlike Mozart, he even got to hear the premiere of his Requiem — Koussevitzky conducted the Boston Symphony — which marked the beginning of a Bartók boom in the States, and established him as the Number One, the leading contemporary composer, including Richard Strauss and Sergei Prokofiev. He returned to New York, to his two-room apartment, and died. — My mother's big uncle didn't survive the war either. The barking of the Fascists could be heard everywhere, and his son barked the loudest. — Boris was now the lord of I Leoni. (Her two little uncles were too fond of the grappa, and her aunt would flit through the corridors in black.) Boris had got fat and smiled wryly. He drove every day in his father's Jaguar to Alba, where he would sit on a Renaissance chair in the salon of a crumbling sixteenth-century *palazzo* and, among the cobwebs and badly torn curtains, hang on every word of a lady who wasn't exactly young. She had steel-blue eyes, dyed blond hair, horsey teeth, and was Anastasia, the daughter of the last Russian Czar. That's what Boris believed, at least, and it could be that the false Anastasia thought she was genuine also. What other explanation was there for her shrieking laughter, the Imperialist way she moved, the divine way she would put her teacup down on the table. Little by little, Boris gave her all his money, and more. Together, they wanted to regain possession of the Czar's riches. Anastasia had promised Boris half of the Amber Room as his reward. That more than offset the fortune he could see vanishing in his beloved's pouch. I Leoni, of course, was going downhill, now no one was making sure everything was okay. Grasses and bushes were sprouting from the windows in the tower again, nettles were growing profusely on the terrace, and the wine, too, tasted again like it did in the days of I Cani when the gods of their foes held sway. The Negro, back then, hadn't quite managed to defeat them, and now they were gaining revenge. Boris was walking on air. He knew the Czar's daughter—he, *he* was the one she preferred to all others! He would be rich, immensely rich, richer than anyone had ever been in the province of Piedmont and much further field.—Edwin had used the war to take care of the company. Immediately after Hitler invaded Poland, he had elected himself President of the Board of Directors—seventy-three per cent of the share capital belonged to him, after all—and turned out to be a strategically active and gifted entrepreneur. The first thing he did was to recruit a leading military figure as the operational head, a brigadier who was allotted to the General Staff—that is, was at its disposal—and took mainly to do with the Spiritual Defence of the nation. He knew about leadership and opened up doors for the firm. He was immediately answerable to Edwin, was his right-hand man, more or less, or executive arm, and soon something of a friend. He would sit, at least, now and then, not too often, by Edwin's fireside, smoking a Havana (where, in the middle of the war, did Edwin get Havana cigars?) and drinking a Mouton Clos du Roi from well before the war. Edwin had enough bottles of the stuff for a thirty years' war. Every morning at seven, the brigadier was expected to report to Edwin—daily sales, the number of orders, redefinitions of longer-term goals, any hitches too—and he received his order of the day. For this, Edwin sat at his desk, attentive, serious. Behind him gleamed the lake. The brigadier stood. (His uniform he wore only if he had to go to Berne that day. He'd to take care, nevertheless, not to click his heels when Edwin, with a nod, dismissed him.) The war opened up markets for the Productions Department to such a degree that a lesser man than Edwin would have felt dizzy. Switzerland's own army, but also the German Wehrmacht, had a huge need for machines of all kinds. The Swiss *réduit* was gobbling tons of metal, and you couldn't get enough vehicle floors or carrying axles for the Germans' Russian campaign. Edwin, however, was not in the least dizzy, he found a new lease of life, marched along the corridors at the double and entered offices without knocking. Woe betide any employee who happened to be dreaming at the window! — He spent animated evenings with Federal Councillors and the General. No mobilization order was ever given without him being consulted. Productivity and Fitness for National Service ended up at loggerheads every time. 'Ah, Edwin,' the General cried one memorable evening in March 1943, in a salon of the Schweizerhof in Berne, where they were drinking cognac. *'Si je vous écoutais, ma petite armée n'aurait plus de soldat du tout!'* Both laughed heartily, and even Federal Councillor Kobelt, who was returning from the loo and only heard the end of the General's joke, joined in the laughter. — The firm grew so rapidly that already in the second year of the war it was operating at full capacity and Edwin had to outsource the production of a variety of parts to small- and medium-sized businesses as far away as the Baselbiet and Jura regions. These often had employees who worked better than those in the parent factory; in the Jura, especially, you could be dismissed, word had it, for being even a tenth of a millimetre out. More by chance — the first time, it simply happened — Edwin noticed that this kind of business immediately got into the most terrible difficulty if, from one day to the next, he withdrew a major order. He could then buy it for a song. The first time, it was the Hänni heirs in Gelterkinden, in the Canton of Basel-Landschaft, a family business that, before the war, had produced light metal window frames and door handles, and then switched, as one of the firm's suppliers, to standardized aluminium parts. Edwin, also more by chance, received a much better offer from Stiner AG in Wangen, in the Canton of Berne, and awarded them the contract instead. That was it for Hänni's heirs. In the end, they—the two brothers, their wives and five children—were even grateful to Edwin for buying the company, if for a price well below its estimated value, and not abandoning them to the fate of misery and bankruptcy. Edwin went on to try this system several times. Each time it worked. With the result that the firm, which itself had expanded to include three more buildings, was surrounded at the end of the war by a ring of highly productive satellites, a number of which produced real specialities. Minimized ball bearings, fine screw thread on the slimmest of bolts, or steel girders that weighed a few grams and yet would hold a train weighing almost a ton. As per 31 December 1945, the firm recorded a turnover of almost ten times what it had been in 1939. Edwin, already rich then, was very rich now. (His wife, who wasn't interested in money as long as some was available, bought one painting after another, fabulous Cézannes, and Alberto Giacometti's *Homme à la pipe*.) He fired the brigadier with a great deal of ceremony and the greatest of honours, and got himself a civilian director of operations, a manager from the merchant bank—He hadn't been able to work much with the orchestra. Too many musicians having to do military service, too many of the audience likewise. And so, throughout the entire war, there were only two concerts on the radio—with conventional programmes that didn't shy away from even Tchaikovsky's *Swan Lake* waltzes—and a concert for the families of soldiers, the programme for which was even more traditional, closing with the national anthem, for which everybody stood.—After the war, Edwin resumed the concerts of the Young Orchestra. The musicians were all in good health, living with the war across the border had been taxing, but not fatal. (That said, the leader of the orchestra was missing, as was the cellist.) The rush for tickets, even before the first concert, was so great—people had been starved of music—that Edwin asked to be allowed to play in the Stadthalle. That venue was the refuge of the Philharmonic, whose conductor, the bone-dry music officer, plotted and schemed with all his might against Edwin and his orchestra. He spoke of the desecration of a place with great tradition—Weingartner and Furtwängler had conducted here—if the cacophonous music of the Bergs and Schönbergs of this world were to be performed. But Edwin was given the room nonetheless, and the very same conditions applied as for the Philharmonic. Six Thursdays and six Fridays per season. And so the first post-war concert was held in the Stadthalle, on 13 September 1945. Mozart, Symphony No. 29 in A major; the Double Concerto for Strings, Piano and Timpani by Bohuslav Martinu; and the Petite symphonie concertante for Harp, Harpsichord, Piano and two String Orchestras by Frank Martin. My mother now sat in the balcony, in the front row at the centre, well away from Edwin. Between him and her, far below, lay the abyss of the stalls. Heads, a thousand heads. When Edwin walked onto the stage, when the audience applauded, when the lights went down and everyone listened without a stir, she had the urge, like before, to scream. Like in the days when she'd sat beside her father and everyone else, her father too, had looked dead. Now she was afraid of herself being dead. But she didn't scream. She stared down and saw Edwin, how — as sparingly as ever — he brought in the musicians. The Mozart was magnificent, the Martinu loud and the Martin piece soon had her dreaming so much, she didn't hear a thing and didn't even notice that the harpist was the young woman Edwin was hugging in the photo from Paris. She had aged; she had, too. — She enjoyed the interval, my mother, at least. 'Good day, Frau Doktor! Good evening, Herr Professor!' They were all back again, and many returned her greeting. Professor von den Steinen, a medievalist and anthroposophist, even stopped, asked how things were. My mother was over-joyed. — The applause at the end was great. Edwin nodded, as ever. When he returned to the stage for the fourth time, he signalled to the orchestra, with a slight hand gesture, to stand, to show their appreciation. They all rose and stood with their instruments in their hands. Only then did my mother notice that throughout the entire concert, on the seat of her friend, the cellist, a young man with a pale face had been sitting; her successor.

MY mother's manner was now no longer to stand in the corner like a piece of firewood, as she'd done as a child. In a fever of excitement, with clenched fists, her eyes turned inwards, imagining kings and murderers whose victim and ruler she was. She no longer skipped in her bright inner land-scapes while the outer shell she left behind, on earth, stood inelegantly in the corner. No. Her manner was now to be exactly like other people. Normal. Indeed,—because she could distinguish perfectly between a rule and its exception— she was more normal than normal people. Unlike them, she didn't ever permit herself a slight short cut, a break, a moment to catch breath, instead she always always took the prescribed route. She was more exact than those famous for being exact, and more punctual than those who were always punctual. (She herself didn't see things that way. In her own eyes, she was never perfect enough. No skin, neither a stranger's, nor least of all her own, could be so pure that it didn't contain some impurity or other.) If she made beds, that was them made for the rest of eternity. If she greeted someone—'Good day, Herr Professor! Good evening, Frau Doktor!'—her smile was just that little bit warmer than that of the person responding, her head was bowed that little bit more. (In her dreams, she was different. She dreamt—or was it her child that dreamt this?—that her child ate his own heart because he was afraid of what his mother fed him. It had gone mad, the child, my mother had a child who was mad, even the police already knew, the neighbours, everyone. She dreamed her child dreamed blood was dripping from her gob.) She now talked a lot, all the time, actually, and loudly. She always stood too close to people. With the result that everyone — be it a man or a woman, a child, or even her dog — would immediately take a step back. She, of course, followed right away. She would begin a conversation in the doorway and be far from finished by the time she got to the gate. — Everyone who spoke to her gave up at some point, weary, exhausted. Would agree with everything she said, even the strangest things. She sucked her victims dry, left their shells behind. Won each time. — When alone, she continued to whisper away to herself. She constantly prowled round the house as if she were wearing invisible armour, the hinges of which caused these strange sounds. Like before, she would launch into wild disputes, discussing whatever it was with an invisible man or woman, whose voice and arguments were powerful. Blame, oh, there was so much blame. She didn't give in, the voice didn't either. 'I can't go on!' she'd sob, if the voice was gaining too much of an upper hand. Imposed punishments that were too dreadful. Beat her too terribly. — The different ways of dying she mumbled more than ever to herself now, as if they were a prayer. Hanging, jumping, drowning: there wasn't a form of death she didn't have on her list. And she was still convinced, of course, that she had to take her child with her. A good mother would never do that: leave her child behind, alone. — She also still feared the nights. She would lie with her eyes open in the dark, waiting for her murderer to arrive. — It would have made you cry to see her standing there, a piece of conglomerate that wanted to be granite. You thought you would have to take a hammer to it, this magnetic mountain, if you wanted to smash it to smithereens. Would have to hit it another few blows if the mouth, as expected, didn't stop. Yes, she often said that: 'Me, they'll have to beat to death!' She would laugh, with panic in her eyes. 'I'll never die of my own accord.' She had indeed never even had flu or toothache. Pain was something foreign to her. She didn't feel the heat, the cold. It was now her manner to be in good health, always.

THE days crept by, the years flew by. The trees around the house shot up so much, it was now barely visible from the gate. A cat came into the house, caught its mice, died. My mother took care of the garden, in which fewer and fewer vegetables and more and more flowers were now growing. Ornamental cherry trees, a tulip tree. Lilacs again. Now a man was helping her, Herr Jenny, a customs officer who, in his free time, took care of a dozen local gardens, and got the work done very quickly. Watering the flowers, raking the leaves, eating his sandwiches. He probably also relieved himself at the double, no doubt still talking. Talking, but also being a fast walker, were things he had in common with my mother. She ran around after him, speaking to his back—it looked as if she were always chasing him—while, speaking at the same time, and as loud as the fanfares at the Last Judgement, he replied over his shoulder. Herr Kern was his name; not Herr Jenny. They got on well, Herr Kern and my mother. One day, in a burning hot August, Herr Kern was on his way to the water barrel with two empty watering cans in his hands and my mother at his back when, suddenly, he turned round, and still walking, backwards, looked at my mother with big, round, appalled eyes, and dropped to the ground. Dead. — The dog died too, Jimmy, as did — later — its replacement, Wally. Her husband was suddenly dead too, before he reached an age that men die at. She buried him, but not in the family grave. Her father wouldn't have wanted it. Many mourners came to the funeral; a great many. Most of them, she didn't know. — She didn't want to visit I Leoni any more, with her big uncle no longer there. She persuaded Boris to let her use the stone dwelling in the summer weeks, and cleared all the junk out. All the dusty empty bottles, the broken crates, the cartwheels, and runners for the sleighs. She brushed and cleaned until the house, more like a cave, was shining like back in the Negro's day. She left everything as it was in his day, the age of the sumpter mules, of the young father. She cooked by candlelight and left the door open during the day to see at least a bit better. She collected wood in the forest, chopped it on a base behind the house. She pumped for water. She slept on a narrow mattress that lay on duckboards. Often, almost every day actually, she climbed a mountain that rose before her, a peak without a name that the locals called 'il Cattivo', 'the Evil One'. It had never done anyone any harm, though; looked threatening only with heavy clouds above it; and by geological coincidence, looked as if it had crafty eyes and an eternal crooked grin. It was as if it had advance knowledge of a disaster that would happen right now, or tomorrow or in a thousand years. My mother climbed the Cattivo so often, a path emerged between her door and the peak, a groove. — She now used the dwelling every summer, she no longer travelled anywhere else. — She was later also exiled from this piece of *Heimat*, — when Boris went bankrupt and had to cede I Leoni to his greatest rival. (Anastasia had long since vanished, together with all the money he'd invested in her and the Amber Room, — and Boris' greatest rival had taken advantage of the years of neglect by seducing his secretary, persuading her, once and for all, to come to his bed, and bring all the records with her.) Boris then gave cultivating truffles a go for a while, but his pigs didn't find anything, or ate the precious nodules before he could restrain them. Then, for two seasons, he ran a swimming pool in Nervi. He was the manager, or rather: a kind of pool attendant who also sold ice-cream and lemonade. Finally, he resorted, in a last revolt, to real estate. He was now carrying fat bundles of bank notes around again — not his own money — and extolling to German investors the virtues of houses that, even during his sales pitch, threatened to collapse. Once, he ended up in court — it was to do with money laundering — had to give evidence, was red in the face, was sweating buckets, became embroiled in contradictions of his own making and yet emerged scot-free. At that point, he decided to retire to Villa di Domodossola, to the stone dwelling; he'd no other home to return to. He had nothing any more, except his Jaguar, that gave up the ghost as soon as it pulled up outside the dwelling. The fuel pump was broken, and Boris hadn't the money to have a new one sent from England. He and my mother in the same house? For the few summer weeks, that might have worked out. Boris, though, was accompanied by my mother's aunt and two little uncles, each of whom immediately made themselves at home, each in a different corner. Unaware of any of this, my mother arrived at the dwelling with bag and baggage just as her uncles were gathering around the jointly owned grappa bottle to celebrate their own arrival. Her aunt stared like a bird. Boris, with a crooked smile, said he was sorry not to be able to drive her back to the station; the fuel pump, if it weren't for that. Her two uncles just stood there, leaning one against the other, grinning. My mother took her case and left. The tags had become so pale, she was the only one able to read them. Suvretta: like a premonition. Danieli, a reminder of very different times. — She now stayed in the house at the edge of the town, in the summers also. For a long time now, it had no longer been at the edge of town, had been surrounded by new houses. Where the crops had been, were now gardens with high hedges and little access roads with turning areas at the end. — Three, four, times, she couldn't take it any more and went into a psychiatric clinic that she herself never called that. It was a different one each time. The University Clinic, Münchenbuchsee, Heiligholz, Sonnenberg. She was given medication that made her go quiet. Not a word. Her steps not entirely steady, she walked along the corridors and across the gravel paths. She floated rather, she wasn't really walking, and her eyes swam past her visitors' gazes. She didn't get any more electric shocks. And still, she couldn't cry, not a single tear. — She attended every concert of the Young Orchestra. She now looked more and more like a queen in exile, a Queen mother, a lady whose face was powdered, stern, with a certain charm. She enjoyed the concerts, didn't miss a single highlight. Arthur Honegger's *Jeanne au bûcher*! *Idomeneo*, with the wonderful Ernst Haefliger! Schönberg's *Pierrot Lunaire*! All the new composers, Wolfgang Fortner, for example, who bowed powerfully, like a German. Stockhausen! Kelterborn! Wildberger! And Bartók, again and again Bartók. Oh, they were beautiful, the concerts of the Young Orchestra. — Then came the birthday, on which Edwin didn't send an orchid. No small card, on which was written, in purple ink, 'All the best, E.' My mother stood at the window, staring across at the gate. Today, this birthday, was terrible, quite terrible, the worst in years, for years. — Later still, she started doing strange things. She would sit down for a rest, an old lady now, on the tracks of the suburban line. The driver — the track was clearly visible — brought his train to a stop and helped her up the embankment. She was pleased he helped her, and laughed. She would now stand at the lake again, from time to time, would take a few steps into it; no longer as far as before. She crossed streets when and where she wanted, never stopping to look left or right. Not even the screeching of brakes or tooting of horns, the sound of metal being bashed or of glass smashing, would throw her. Once she had become really old, she starting going off on journeys — the more dangerous, the more attractive — and went all round eastern Turkey, for example, by bus. On one occasion, all the passengers had to duck behind earthwork because Turks were shooting at Kurds, or vice versa; across the top of their bus, in any case. My mother crouched beside a young man who was as white as chalk, and gave him a wink. She was in New York, too, and set off every day, in a rain-proof jacket and shoes that looked like a duck's feet, to explore the Bronx or Brooklyn or the city subway. She always had a ten-dollar bill in her right anorak pocket, as someone had advised her to do, in case she was mugged. 'There you go, young man!,' she would have said, had that ever happened—she'd practised the sentence carefully—and given him the money. But she was never mugged. Once, in Harlem, in a bar in a side street of Third Avenue, she had a cup of tea, standing at the counter. It was a gay bar, a black gay bar, and my mother was served with much merriment. Her English sounded the way her teacher had once imagined the English in Oxford to sound. 'There you go, young man,' she said when she paid.

ON 17 February 1987, my mother made her bed in the old people's home where she now lived, straightened the little silver bowls and candlesticks, and wrote on a piece of paper, 'I can't go on any more. Live and laugh. Clara.' Her writing now resembled the flapping of birds that are hurting. My mother opened the window—she lived on the sixth floor—and looked across, once more, to the other shore, gleaming in the sun. 'Edwin,' she said. Then she jumped. She screamed now, I think. 'Edwin.' Deep within, all she'd suffered in her eighty-two years, or the bawling at the beginning, raged. The rush of wind made her eyes water. 'Edwin!' She hit the roof of the caretaker's car, a Fiat 127. She was wearing just one shoe, the other—one of those duck shoes—had caught on the window frame and remained there as she flung herself out.— There was a funeral service, in a hall at the municipal cemetery. A few of her female friends, her child. Me. No clergy. She, who always wanted to do things the way others did them, wanted nothing to do with the clergy. So no one spoke. The first First Violist of the Young Orchestra—he'd long since ceased to be part of it; he, too, was an old man now—played a Bach piece with trembling fingers. No wreath from Edwin. No card, no purple ink. The coffin suddenly rolled, without warning and without fanfare, through a hatch that opened abruptly, into the fire, into which everyone stared, with horror in their hearts. The hatch closed again. The few mourners got up, looked around to see if they recognized anyone, and then went home, somehow.—The urn with my mother's ashes was brought to the family grave, up on the redoubts, a few days later. To her left is her father's urn, the space to her right is still free.—The caretaker, whose Fiat had been dented, fought for almost a year with my dead mother's insurers. The compensation paid to him, he reckoned, was too little.

THE story has been told. The story of a passion, a stubborn passion. A requiem. A bow to a life that was hard to live. This, by way of addition, perhaps: recently, barely a week ago, I was in the Ethnological Museum to see Wern's collection. I strolled through the exhibition rooms, gazed in wonder at wild demons' masks and admired the reconstruction of the hut of a distinguished man, probably Wern himself. It's true the hammock wasn't made of gold, there was no hammock at all, in fact, but in a wooden bowl lay two cigars, hand rolled, and long dried-out, no doubt, that were very similar to Wern's. A table, two stools, raffia mats. Jewellery, probably that of the princess. Wooden dinner services, too, and wooden spoons. Clay pots, beautifully decorated. — I was alone in the museum. Silence, complete silence; dim light from high windows. Only when I reached the room with the house for men — a large installation, occupying all of one side — did I see another visitor, an old man, who was marvelling at a *kṣatrya*, a larger-than-life black bull made of something like papier maché, used for the burials of great people. A kind of magic coffin. The man was so small beneath the huge animal, it looked as if the sacred monster wanted to devour him. Both stood there, neither flinching, a demon and a man. A dialogue between the two? A prayer? A test of strength? Suddenly I recognized the old man. Edwin. Edwin had aged, was ancient; but anything but frail. He skipped, virtually, when he freed himself from the monster's spell, and went over to a grotesque wooden face that looked less dangerous. I wandered from exhibit to exhibit until I was standing beside Edwin. He was looking at a canoe, meanwhile, that had the snout of a crocodile, and in which lay two oars and three water bottles fashioned from pumpkins. I had never seen Edwin from so close. He didn't only have the nose of a bird of prey, —no, his eyes, too, were keen and attentive. He'd long since noted my presence, of course, and now gave me a quick glance, from the side. His neck was full of wrinkles, round which was tied an immaculate white scarf.

'I am Clara's son,' I said.

'Whose son?' He continued to look at the crocodile disguised as a ship.

'Clara's'—I used her name from back then—'Clara Molinari.'

He turned to me. 'Clara Molinari?' he said. 'I can't say, right now, that that name's familiar to me. I meet so many people.'

'I beg your pardon!' I shouted, annoyed suddenly. 'Clara was the first honorary member of your Orchestra! You won't have forgotten that, I take it?'

Edwin slapped his forehead, saying, 'But of course! Good old Clara. How is she then?'

'She's dead.'

'Yes.' He nodded. 'More and more of us are.'

He pointed to the house for men, the bull and the crocodile canoe, a large gesture, that took the whole room in. 'Most interesting culture. Very complex, extremely efficient network based on kinship. Patrilineal, but with women dominating strongly.' He felt for his scarf and straightened it.

'Why did you stop sending Clara orchids?' I said.

'Orchids?'

'Yes. With a small card. Purple ink. "All the best, E." I can still see it, your handwriting, as if it were yesterday.'

'Things like that are dealt with by the office.' Edwin shrugged, apologetically. 'A new secretary probably tidied up my diary.'

I nodded. Yes. As an explanation it was plausible. I said nothing more. The conversation seemed to have ended for Edwin, too, for he was rushing across to a cabinet full of demonic heads of pigs and sheep.

'Another thing,' I called across when he got there, 'Why did you force Clara to abort her child? Your child?'

'Who told you that?' Between him and me now lay twenty, or even thirty, metres of parquet flooring, and his voice echoed. 'I don't force any woman to do anything. Not ever. I have four children. And I have always been generous to the mothers. Extremely generous.'

I went over to him quickly, with steps that sounded like rifle shots. I wanted, possibly, to slap him, or to kick him between the legs, or at least roar at him. 'I have heard all of your concerts,' I said, instead, when I got there. 'All the Bartóks, the *Idomeneo* you did back then. Liebermann! Hartmann! Zimmermann! Wonderful.' My voice—as loud and almost as high as my mother's—at most gave away the fact my right hand and my right foot were still twitching and trembling.—He now smiled. Inhaled, exhaled. Yes, he really was beaming. 'The day after tomorrow,' he said, 'I have a concert. Ligeti, Bartók, Beck. Come along, do come along!' He gave me a friendly slap on the cheek, turned away, and took quick, confident steps towards the exit. He disappeared in the darkness of the doorway, and I was just about to turn to the pig and dog masks when he turned up again, his face blushing with pleasure. 'If your story were accurate,' he called over to me, giggling, 'that would make you *my* son!' He raised both arms and dropped them again. 'Bad luck, young man.'

He disappeared so quickly, he didn't see me tapping my forehead with my index finger. 'You must think nothing happens without you being involved?' I roared. I then just stood there, listening to his footsteps dying away. His laughter becoming less and less audible. A door banged shut, and it was silent again. The demons were all silent as they had been for centuries already. Only the bull in the house for the men, the *ksatrya*, now appeared to be laughing, so silently, and with such an echo, that I too left the museum.

MY mother's lover was carried to his grave today. I had been delayed—though it made no sense, I'd washed my shirts before leaving—and I arrived at the Grossmünster only after the service had already begun. The entire square outside was filled with mourners who had not been admitted to the cathedral. Thousands, the square all in black, as far as the guild houses at the other end. I managed nonetheless to get inside, pushing, and using my elbows. I got no further than a solid, Romanesque pillar, and had to stand on tiptoe to see anything at all. In the nave sat ladies in black hats and veils, so motionless, *they* might have been the dead; and gentlemen, many of whom had a top hat on their knees. Up at the front, way up the front, were the dignitaries, many in uniform. A few federal councillors, presumably, those responsible for the economy and culture. From so far back, I couldn't see them properly. The Bodmer, Lermitier and Montmollin representatives were, of course, in the front row. Thanks to her white hair, I recognized the doyenne of the Montmollin family, a centenarian, of whom it is said even rattlesnakes take to their heels when they see her. By the time I'd forced my way through to the baptism font, the president of the Federal Council was speaking. I had a good view. He acknowledged that, without the music of the twentieth century, his life would have been poorer. The Young Orchestra, older now, played Mozart's Masonic Funeral Music and something Bach-like I didn't know. The conductor I couldn't see, however. The pulpit was concealing him such that I could only see his right arm, the one with the baton, and only at those moments when he wanted to spur the orchestra on to a very intense emotion. If it wasn't Pierre Boulez, it was probably Heinz Holliger or perhaps Wolfgang Rihm. Someone close to the younger generation, anyhow. —After the final piece of music, a transparently modern cry of anguish involving all the wind instruments, by a contemporary composer, no doubt — perhaps even the conductor, wild applause erupted, a faux pas that took everyone so much by surprise that, continuing to clap, they even stood up to give the dead man a standing ovation. I'd been standing a long time already, it's true, but I clapped too, though I don't know why. I clapped until my hands were sore. There was no end to the clapping—though the coffin, buried under the flowers, didn't take a bow—and in the end, the pastor in the Grossmünster, an elderly man with a kind smile, had to put an end to it by waving. The mourners' faces were all flushed, their eyes shining, like after an especially splendid concert.—When I left the cathedral, it was pouring. A sea of black umbrellas. The whole town wanted to accompany the deceased on his way to the cemetery. I don't know which. I went home, even before the hearse, a black Mercedes with white curtains, started to move. The cathedral bells were ringing; those of all the other local churches were ringing, too.—Later, I sat in front of the TV for a few hours and watched the special tribute broadcast to mark Edwin's death. The stations of his life. His trials and triumphs. 'One of the century's most important figures.' I saw Edwin with Bartók, Edwin with Stravinsky, Edwin with the young Queen of England and, at one point, as the camera panned over the Stadthalle audience, I saw, at the centre of the balcony,—from far off, and for just a fraction of a second—a shadow that may well have been my mother.